THE
THREE
ROADS

Ross Macdonald

BANTAM BOOKS
TORONTO · NEW YORK · LONDON · SYDNEY

THE THREE ROADS

*A Bantam Book / published by arrangement with
Alfred A. Knopf, Inc.*

PRINTING HISTORY

*Knopf edition published June 1948
Bantam edition published June 1960
2nd printing . . . March 1968
New Bantam edition published August 1974
2nd printing . . . August 1974
3rd printing . . . September 1974
4th printing . . . June 1983*

THE PUNISHING SATISFACTION OF PAIN

"Come on and fight like a man, you friggin' coward!" The sentence was punctuated by a blow on the side of the head which sent Bret reeling. He came back to attack the red face behind the fists.

A left jab to the cheek and a right across to the side of the jaw put Mustin on his back. Bret stood over the fallen man, pleased to see the blood on his face. He heard a sound in the air behind and over his head, but it was too late to duck. A hard blow jolted the back of his head and split the room into many tiny fragments. It must have been a bottle, he thought as his knees buckled and he fell forward onto the floor. Then the black wind blew out the fluorescent lights. . . .

CONTENTS

For now am I discovered vile, and of the vile. O ye three roads, and thou concealed dell, and oaken copse, and narrow outlet of three ways, which drank my own blood . . .

SOPHOCLES, *Oedipus Tyrannus*

PART I

SATURDAY

CHAPTER ONE

From the veranda where she had been left to wait she could see the golf course adjoining the hospital grounds. Along the distant hillside, still green from the winter rains, a tiny man in faded suntans was chasing an invisible ball. She had been watching him for some time before she noticed that he handled his club in an unusual way. He was teaching himself to play golf with one hand. She hoped he had been left-handed to begin with.

She forgot the tiny man when she heard Bret's footsteps behind her. He turned her toward him, holding her by the shoulders in a grip that almost hurt and studying her face. Looking up into his calm eyes, she understood the doubt that lay behind them. She felt it in her own mind whenever she came to see him after a week's absence, uncertain and bereft, like a relative called upon to identify the victim of a drowning.

Bret hadn't really changed, but he had taken on weight during his nine months in the hospital. It had altered the lines of his cheek and jaw and made his old gray uniform seem too small for him. She could never wholly free her mind of the suspicion that this Bret Taylor was an impostor, living a healthy vegetative life

3

in a dead man's clothes, battening on the love she owed to the man that was lost.

She shivered against him, and he tightened his arms around her. She had no right to such fantastic notions. It was her job to bring reality to him. She was his interpreter of the outside world, and she mustn't forget its language. But even with his arms round her she was chilled by the old terror. During the first few minutes of their meetings she always skated on the thin ice at the edge of sanity. Her whole concern was to keep her feelings from showing in her face.

Then he kissed her. The contact was re-established and drew her back to her emotional center. The lost man had been found and was in her arms.

The orderly who had accompanied Bret as far as the door reminded them of his presence. "You want to stay out here, Miss West? It gets kind of chilly in the afternoons."

She looked at Bret with the deference that had become instinctive with her. Since he had no large decisions to make, let him make all the small ones.

"Let's stay out here," he said. "If you get cold we can go in."

She smiled at the orderly, and he disappeared. Bret placed two deck chairs side by side, and they sat down.

"And now I'd like a cigarette," she said. The case in her bag was full, but she preferred to have one of his. Apart from the fact that it was his, which was important, it helped build up the illusion of casualness and freedom.

"They always call you Miss West," he said when he lit her cigarette.

"Inasmuch as that's my name—"

"But it isn't your real name?"

For a moment she was afraid to look at him, afraid that his mind had reverted to the time when he didn't know her. But she replied in a sweetly reasonable voice: "Well, no, it isn't. I explained to you that I started to work in Hollywood under my maiden name. I never use my married name except on checks."

"I didn't remember," he said humbly.

"Nobody can remember everything. I've even forgotten my own telephone number."

"I've forgotten my own name. My memory's getting better though."

"I know it is, every time I come."

He said with sober pride, like an explorer announcing the discovery of a new island: "I remembered Kerama Retto the other night."

"Really? That's the news of the week."

"The news of the year for me. I remembered the whole thing. It was so real I thought it was happening over again. I could see the rice paddies above the harbor in the glare of the explosion. It was so bright it blinded me."

She was dismayed by his sudden pallor. Along his hairline there was a row of minute sweat drops that the February sun did not account for.

"Don't talk about it if it's painful, darling."

He had turned away and was looking across the lawn, which sloped down from the veranda into the valley holding the sunshine like a lake of light. Its very peace, she thought, must make it seem more dreamlike to his unpeaceful mind than the remembered terraces of that island off Japan.

The silence between them was too full of echoes, and she broke it with the first words that entered her head. "I had fruit salad for lunch. I had to wait twenty minutes to get into the dining-room, but they do make good fruit salad at the Grant."

"Do they still put avocado in it?"

"Yes."

"I bet you didn't eat the avocado."

"It's always been too rich for me," she answered happily. He was remembering everything again.

"We had avocado salad for lunch on Wednesday or Thursday. No, it was Wednesday, the same day I had my hair cut."

"I like you with your hair cut short. I always have."

The direct compliment embarrassed him. "It's convenient for swimming anyway. I didn't tell you I was swimming on Thursday."

"No, I didn't know."

"I expected to be afraid of the water, but I wasn't. I swam under water the full length of the pool. I soon get tired of swimming in a pool though. I'd give anything to get into the surf again."

"Would you really? I'm so glad."

"Why?"

"Oh, I don't know. I may have had an idea you'd hate the sea."

"I hated the idea of it for a while, but I don't any more. Anyway I could never hate La Jolla."

The happiness inside her pressed tears into her eyes. La Jolla had only one meaning for her; it was the place where they had met. "Remember the day the seals came in?" She winced at her word "remember." It was always coming up, like the word "see" when one was talking to a blind man.

He leaned forward abruptly in his chair, his hunched shoulder muscles stretching his uniform tight. Have I made a mistake? she thought in terror. It was so hard to preserve her balance between a soothing therapeutic attitude and the irrational love she felt for him.

All he said was: "We'll have to go back there together—soon. It seems incredible that it's only fifteen miles from here."

"I know you'll be able to go soon. You're getting so much better."

"You honestly think so?"

"You know you are."

"Some days I feel perfectly well," he said slowly. "I can hardly wait to get back to work. Then my mind comes to a blank space, and I feel as if I'm back where I started. Have you ever imagined a total vacuum? A place where there's no air, no light, no sound?

Not even darkness, not even silence. I guess it's death my mind comes up against. I guess I'm partly dead."

She put her hand over his taut fingers, which were gripping the arm of his chair. "You're very much alive, Bret. You're making a perfect comeback." But his gloomy tension alarmed her and set her thinking. What if she wasn't good for him? What if he'd be better off without her? No, that couldn't be true. The doctor had told her more than once that she was just what he needed, that she gave him something to live for.

"It's taking a long time," he said. "Sometimes I wonder if I'll ever get out of this place. Sometimes, I don't really want to. I feel a little bit like Lazarus. He couldn't have been very happy when he came back and tried to take up his life where he left off."

She told him sharply: "You mustn't talk like that. Your life isn't half over, darling. You've only been ill for less than a year."

"It feels as long as prehistoric time." He had enough humor to smile at his own hyperbole.

"Forget the past," she said impulsively.

"I have to remember it first." He smiled again, not a good smile, but it was something.

"You are remembering it. But you can think of the future too."

"I'll tell you what I do think about a good deal of the time."

"What?"

"I think of us together. It's thinking of that that keeps me going. It must be hard for you to be a hospital widow."

"A hospital widow?"

"Yes. It must be hard for a woman to have a husband in a mental ward. I know a lot of women would clear out and get a divorce—"

"But, darling." It would have been so much easier to pass it over or to humor his delusion, but she stuck to the difficult truth. "I'm not your wife, Bret."

He looked at her blankly. "You said you didn't use your married name—"

"My married name is Pangborn. I told you I divorced my husband."

She watched the manhood draining out of his face and could think of no way to rescue it. "I thought we were married," he said in a high, weak voice. "I thought you were my wife."

"You have no wife." She didn't trust herself to say anything more.

He was searching desperately for some excuse, for anything to mitigate his shame. "Are we engaged then? Is that what it was? Are we going to be married?"

"If you will have me." There was no atom of irony in any crevice of her mind.

He got out of his chair and stood awkwardly and miserably in front of her. His blunder had shaken him badly. "I guess it's time for you to go. Will you kiss me good-bye?"

"I'd die if I couldn't."

His mouth was soft and uncertain, and he held her very gently. He left her abruptly then, as if he could not bear to stay with her any longer after his humiliation. She was proud of the way he went back to his room alone, like any normal man retiring to his hotel room, but his mistake had shocked and worried her. She had had him in her grasp for a moment, and then he had slipped away again, to a place where she did not dare to follow.

CHAPTER TWO

Commander Wright raised his arm and pointed across the valley. "See that chap with the golf club?"

Paula heard the words without grasping their meaning. It seemed to her that the afternoon was repeating itself. Her meeting with Bret had only been a rehearsal, and the set was being arranged for a final retake. The tiny man in suntans was pursuing his invisible ball back and forth along the hillside. Soon Bret would come out on the veranda, and he and she would read their lines again. But this time there'd be no mistakes, no hideous sting in the tail of their conversation. She'd have a chance to tell him the good news about Klifter, and they'd part on a note of hopefulness for once.

Then she felt the chilly touch of the wind that always sprang up from the bay in the late afternoons. It brought her back to reality with a pang. Bret had come and gone, and the mistake he had made could not be changed by dreaming.

Wright cocked his finger impatiently and pointed again. The heavy black hair on the back of his hand glistened like iron in the sun. "You see him, don't you?"

"I'm sorry, I wasn't listening. I'm afraid Bret's notion that we were married got me down."

The doctor grunted and shifted his body in the creaking deck chair. "That's precisely what I'm trying to explain. That chap with the golf club has a simple problem compared with Taylor's. He lost an arm, and that's no fun, but he can get along without it. He's only got a physical adjustment to make, and he's doing that now. That's what Taylor would like to do."

"I don't quite see the analogy."

"Taylor would rather suppress certain memories than live with them. He'd rather go armless than grow a new arm. But so long as he suppresses those memories of the past he can't make a healthy adjustment to the present. Past and present are so intertwined that you can't abandon one without losing your grip on the other. Loss of the present is a fair description of insanity."

"But he's not insane!" The words flew out in protest, almost of their own accord.

He turned to smile at her, baring his strong white teeth. "You shouldn't get excited about words, Miss West. They're all relative, especially the ones we use in psychiatry. I think he's listed in the files as 'traumatic neurosis with hysteric symptoms.' Does that suit you better?"

"I have no deep respect for words. They're my business after all. But 'insanity' sounds so hopeless."

"It isn't necessarily hopeless. But I didn't mean to imply that Taylor is insane. Insanity is a legal concept, and from the legal point of view he's compos mentis. He goes through intelligence tests in a breeze. His orientation is still uncertain, but he could probably leave here tomorrow and get along for the rest of his life as well as most."

"Could he really?"

"If he didn't have to face any serious crisis."

"But there seem to be such dreadful gaps in his memory. In some ways he's worse than he was four months ago. He didn't think we were married then."

"I wasn't surprised when that cropped up. He's taken a little step back in order to take a big step forward. Four months ago he refused to admit the possibility that he had been married."

"Doesn't he remember his wife at all?"

"No, but he will. I see a great deal more of him than you do, and I'm honestly not worried by these temporary setbacks. He's on the point of total recovery, and unconsciously he knows it. His mind is fighting that prospect with every weapon at its disposal, and fighting a losing battle."

"You think he doesn't want to get well? He said something like that today."

"Why do you think he became ill in the first place?"

"Isn't it fairly obvious? He had two terrible shocks in rapid succession. The bombing and then his wife's death—"

"Nothing about the human mind is obvious." There was a trace of professional pomposity in his tone, which shortly became more apparent. "As a matter of fact the healthy mind is quite as mysterious as the unhealthy mind. I've often wondered, for instance, why a woman like you—"

His hand, like a fat and hairy spider, was gently approaching hers along the arm of the chair. She withdrew her own hand into her lap. "Since Lieutenant Taylor and I are going to be married—"

The hairy spider stopped in its tracks.

"—I have to ask you whether his brain could have been damaged by the explosion. Physically damaged?"

"Not a chance. It's a purely psychological problem, Miss West. It's hardly oversimplifying it to say that he lost his memory because he wanted to."

"But you've said yourself that the shocks had a great deal to do with it."

"They precipitated his condition, but they're not the basic explanation. Taylor's mind was vulnerable, you see. Other men have endured similar shocks without resorting to mental blackout."

"Resorting?" She picked out the word and threw it back like an insult. She was beginning to hate him again; and she had an impulse to brush the inert and hairy hand from the arm of her chair.

"You're letting words bother you again. I used that word advisedly and without prejudice. He had several years of arduous sea duty, much of it under combat conditions. He took it standing up, like thousands of others. Then he was bombed into the water at Kerama. No doubt that weakened his resistance, both mentally and physically. But he came out of it without any overt mental condition. It was the second shock, coming on top of years of strain, that broke the camel's back."

"You mean her death?"

"Evidently. The murder coincided with his final breakdown. That camel's back isn't a good metaphor. Really his whole image of the world and of himself was strained by a series of hard blows. He finally withdrew from a situation that was too much for him. I can't help feeling that he wanted to escape from it even before she was killed. There's his complete refusal to remember her at all." He looked sideways at her from under his thick brows. "He wasn't happy with her, was he?"

"He hardly knew her. He married her on a three-day furlough and went to sea immediately afterward. He married her in the fall of 1944 and never saw her alive again."

"How on earth did he come to do that?"

She paused to take charge of her feelings. This memory was as painful to her as it must have been to Bret. "He married her when he was drunk. He picked her up in a bar in San Francisco and married her the next day."

"Good Lord, what kind of a girl was she?"

"That kind," she said.

"You knew Taylor at that time, did you?"

"Oh, yes, I knew him." She lit a cigarette in a series of quick, nervous movements and said: "I suppose I'd better tell you about it if you think it might have any bearing. Perhaps I should have told you long ago."

"Why didn't you?"

"It's not an anecdote I tell around for laughs," she said harshly. "When his ship came in to San Francisco I thought he was going to marry me. So did he, I think. I flew up from Hollywood to meet him. He'd been at sea for nearly a year that time, and in spite of his letters it was almost as if he'd risen from the dead. Does that sound romantic? I am a romantic, I suppose, or I was. I was crazy with happiness when he came back. But it turned out that he wasn't. He quarreled with me on the first night and left me flat. The next I heard of him he was married to this girl Lorraine. I thought I was going to be the object of a whirlwind courtship, but it turned out to be somebody else."

"It seems strange that you should quarrel so suddenly and finally. Had you known him long?"

"Less than a year, but it seemed longer. I'd met him in La Jolla the winter before, the winter of '43, when he was on leave. We spent nineteen days together before his ship went out, and then there were his letters. He was my personal stake in the war, and I had the feeling that I was his stake in the future. I counted too heavily on that, I guess."

"What was your quarrel about?"

"It was his quarrel, not mine. He resented my having more money than he had, but it wasn't money that made the trouble. He was looking for an occasion for a fight, and that happened to be it. He called me a few names and walked out. It's occurred to me since that his actions, even then, were a little—a little abnormal. I suppose that's nothing but hindsight."

"Is that why you've forgiven him?"

"Did I say I'd forgiven him?" She threw away her cigarette with a gesture that was unnecessarily fierce. It curved over the veranda railing in a steep parabola and lay smoldering in the grass.

"You evidently have, Miss West. Is it because you feel he was not, shall we say, quite master of himself when he left you?"

She noticed the change in the doctor's tone from the personal to the professional, and it pleased her. His hands had forgotten her and were busy filling his pipe. She lit a new cigarette before she answered, and blew out a cloud of smoke as if to veil the clarity of her thoughts.

"Oh, he was master of himself, all right. He carried on his naval duties for another six months. He even won a commendation off Iwo. My head was bloody but his head was unbowed."

"But you yourself suggested that his conduct was abnormal."

"Maybe it wasn't for him," she said quickly. "I knew from the first that he was terribly shy. He was shy of love, and I may have tried to rush him."

"You must love him very much."

"Because I tried to throw myself at his head?"

"Because you're being so honest," he answered soberly, "telling me of your humiliation because you think it might help him."

"I do seem to be a bear for punishment, don't I? Do you suppose I'm a masochist?"

"I doubt it." His answering smile withdrew his eyes far under the thicket of his eyebrows. "About your theory that he was afraid of love—how does it fit in with this whirlwind courtship of his and his marriage to this girl?"

"I don't pretend to have a theory, doctor. But don't forget he went on a binge when he left me. It may be that alcohol put his inhibitions to sleep. His natural sexual impulses broke through and fastened on the first object that was handy. He didn't come right out with it, but that's what I read between the lines of his letter."

"You corresponded with him afterwards?"

"He wrote me one letter. It came about a month after he left San Francisco again."

"I'd like to see that letter."

"I can tell you what it said. He was too proud to admit that he'd acted like a fool, but that was the general idea. He was sticking with the marriage and doing his best to convince himself that he liked the setup, but he didn't like it at all. There was a false, brittle cheerfulness in the letter that really got me down. He was so obviously unhappy and remorseful and apologetically defiant, if you know what I mean."

"I think I do—one of those letters it's hard to answer."

"I didn't try to answer it. He asked me not to, so I didn't. It was pretty hard for a while. I'd got into the habit of writing him everything I did and thought. Then suddenly he belonged to another woman, and I wasn't even hearing from him any more. I finally broke down and went to see her."

"All the way to San Francisco?"

"She'd bought a house in Los Angeles, and I found her in the phone book. It gave me a queer feeling to see that name in print: 'Mrs. Bret Taylor.'" She paused and lit another cigarette from the butt of the one she had been smoking. When she spoke again, her voice had lost its emotional depth:

"It wasn't curiosity about her so much, but I had to know what was happening to him, and she was the only one who could tell me. He'd been gone for nearly four months, and I hadn't heard from him for three, not since the letter I told you about. I'd taken to lying awake nights. And I suppose one of the things I wondered about was the kind of girl that he'd preferred to me."

"I've been wondering about that myself." He accompanied the indirect compliment with a slow and calculated look that slid from her bosom down her body to her naked legs.

She was too preoccupied to notice. "I had a mean sort of triumph when I saw the girl for the first time. She was pretty enough—I've got to acknowledge that —but she used too much make-up, she didn't know how to dress, she didn't know how to wear her hair. Those are trivial things, but they can mean a good deal to a jilted woman. She wasn't even a good housekeeper. There were used glasses and full ashtrays on the tables and chairs. I shouldn't be catty like this, should I? *Nil nisi bonum.*"

"A touch of the feline is natural enough under the circumstances."

"Anyway I suffered for my little moment of false triumph. She showed me the bundle of letters Bret had sent her, and even insisted that I read one of them. Bret had told her about me, you see, and she was perfectly willing to see me suffer. She was quite sweet to me, but in a deadly way. I didn't want to read the letter, but I'm afraid I did. I felt compelled to.

"It was the sort of thing you write to a child, stiff and reassuring. He was at sea again; he couldn't tell her where, but it was exciting; he loved her and looked forward to seeing her. It was painful to read, but it gave me a certain consolation. He had nothing really to say to her, and she didn't have brains or feeling enough to know the difference."

"I gather she was pretty young." There was in his voice an elegiac undertone that Paula resented in spite of herself.

"Nineteen or twenty, I'd say. She had nearly ten years on me, and that didn't help. But she was no child bride. She went out of her way to let me know she'd been around. Frankly I had the feeling that Bret had been seduced."

"It's fairly evident that someone had to," Wright said quietly.

"I know. I tried to, our last night together, but it didn't take. He was a virgin, and I'd been married before. Yet I'm sure he loved me."

"That may have been precisely the trouble. He's a bit of an idealist, isn't he?"

"You know him."

"He's an idealist all right. And that's all very well, but when idealists break down, and they nearly always do, they tend to go to the opposite extreme. This girl, for instance. I presume his interest in her was primarily sexual. How did she feel about him?"

"I don't believe she had any strong feeling one way or the other, but then I'm not an unbiased witness. She seemed to be proud of being married to a full lieutenant in the Navy, and having a little house of her own, though she wasn't doing much to keep it up. She was a little tight when I got there, quite early in the afternoon. She offered me a bottle of beer, and I tried to get her to talk, but it was heavy going. I'm no giant intellect, but she was a featherbrain. Our only common ground was the movies."

"And Lieutenant Taylor?"

"No, not even Bret. Our conceptions of him were so different I found I couldn't talk with her about him. Not without getting angry, at least, and I certainly wasn't going to do that. To her he was an acquisition, a meal ticket garnished with gold braid. She mentioned twice that he had bought her the house and was sending her an allotment of two hundred dollars a month. In spite of those things I invited her to return my visit, but she never did. I guess I didn't do a very good job of covering my feelings, and she resented me quite as much as I resented her. I called on her about two months before she was murdered, and I didn't see her alive after that."

Wright hammered his pipe on his heel with flagellant intensity. "You didn't see her alive?" he said with his face averted.

"I saw her dead. I was with Bret when he found her body."

He glanced up into her face and was embarrassed by the pain he saw there. "Oh, yes. Of course."

"I told you about it when you took charge of Bret's case. I hope I don't have to go through it again."

"There's no need to," he answered quickly. "We have a complete record."

"As a matter of fact I do have to go through it again," she said. "I've got an appointment with Dr. Klifter tonight."

"Klifter?"

"The psychoanalyst. I assumed that Captain Kelvie

had told you about him. He's agreed to interview Bret tomorrow. With your permission," she added coldly.

"Of course the captain talked to me about it. The name slipped my mind for a moment."

"A Freudian error, Commander?"

"Not at all. I've read Klifter's monographs, and I think they're fine. But it's hard to get used to the idea that he's in California. He's always been a sort of European myth to me."

"He's a very charming and unpretentious man," Paula said. "He acted as technical adviser on a script I rewrote—that's how I happen to know him. I'll be very glad if he consents to take the case. I take it you have no objections to his interviewing Bret?"

"None at all. Since you have the captain's permission, mine's only a formality anyway. Actually I'll be glad of the chance to discuss the case with Klifter. I do want to warn you though not to expect too much."

"I expect very little."

"I don't mean that Taylor won't recover, and I don't mean that psychoanalysis mightn't be useful. Our pentothal interview is a variation of psychoanalytic technique, as a matter of fact."

"I know that." She rose to go, holding her purse before her body like a shield. She had worn, for Bret's eyes, a woolen dress that clung to the outlines of her shoulders and breasts. "I'll miss my train."

"Let me take you down in the station wagon."

"Thank you, I have a cab waiting."

"All I meant," he repeated as she offered him her hand, "was that you mustn't look for a sudden miracle. These things take time. Nothing can take the place of time."

She heard his final sentence two ways. The meaning that echoed in her mind all the way to the station was the one he had not intended. Time was running away like a river, and she and Bret were lodged on opposite banks. Nothing could take the place of the time that had already run out or the time that was yet to run.

CHAPTER THREE

Although she had passed between them uncounted
times, Paula was always struck by the contrast between the Santa Fe station and the San Diego gas
company building. The latter was an ugly huge cube
of a building, surrounded by towering steel chimneys
like candles on a birthday cake. Across the streetcar
tracks was the archaic and sentimental incongruity of
the station tower. It seemed to her that the two buildings were symbols of historic forces. On the one hand
was the giant mass of the power and utility companies
that actually dominated the life of the state; on the
other, the Spanish past that California plutocracy used
to stucco its façade.

The shining metal streamliner waiting beside the
station added the final touch to her allegory. It was the
impossible future superimposed upon the ugly present
in the presence of the regretted past. There was no
continuity between the tenses, she thought. You
passed from one to the other as a ghost passed through
a wall, at the risk of your own reality. The spotless interior of this streamlined future was crowded with unreal passengers waiting to be transported, appropriate-
ly enough, to Los Angeles.

She moved like a sleepwalker along the platform
and found the chair she had reserved in the parlor car.
Even the train's starting, one of her oldest excite-

19

ments, and the blue glimpses of the sea as they passed outside the city, failed to lift her out of her mood of vague resignation. After her five years in California there was still something false and garish about summer weather in February. She'd have preferred an unsmiling sky and a gray sea to that steady yellow sun and those glittering waves. She wondered if there was anything in the idea she'd heard somewhere that too much fair weather could make people hard-hearted and self-indulgent.

On an afternoon like this, and with a parlor car to observe it from, it was hard to believe in sin and madness and death. That cotton-batting surf didn't look much like cruel, crawling foam. But of course it was, and people suffered in California just as they did in other places—suffered a little more, perhaps, because they didn't get much sympathy from the weather.

She forced blankness on her mind, smiled as an act of faith, and watched the belt of orange trees that had appeared between the railroad and the sea. A sailor passing in the aisle, willing and eager to accept her blind smile as a personal tribute, paused beside her chair.

"Good afternoon," he said with the assurance of extreme youth and a double row of ribbons. "A lovely afternoon, isn't it?"

As if he were appraising an object on which he intended to enter a bid, he stood and frankly examined her polished-copper hair, her smooth skin, the promise of the figure revealed by her blue wool dress. She couldn't bring herself to feel angry. She was on the brink of thirty, and she'd never been quite beautiful enough to be smug about her looks. On the other hand she wasn't going to listen to wolfish chatter all the way to Los Angeles.

"Blow, swabbie," she whispered hoarsely. "My husband's an officer."

"Certainly, certainly." He tipped his white hat forward onto the bridge of his nose, and said before he strolled away: "No hard feelings."

She turned back to the orange groves rushing by like a dark green river on which thousands of tiny oranges floated dizzily away. She was worried about the lie she had told, not because it was a lie, but because she had claimed Bret Taylor as her husband. He wasn't, and she was afraid he never would be. He'd turned her down in San Francisco in no uncertain terms, and if she'd had any pride she'd have given up when he married the other girl. Yet here she was, nearly two years later, still camping on his trail and beginning to tell strangers on trains that she was his wife. She'd have to watch herself or she'd be going around making all sorts of extravagant claims, like the old woman in Monterey who said she was Mary the Mother of God.

Her real embarrassment came from a deeper source. In the two and a half years since she had met Bret Taylor there had been stirrings in the heart of her body as heavy and ultimate as seismic movements. She had to admit that she was beginning to feel as female as hell, as female and irrational as any D. H. Lawrence *Fräulein*. She wanted a man and she wanted a child. Yet she felt that it was faintly ridiculous to be an old-maid Rachel weeping over her unborn children. After all, she had been married and knew the answers, most of which were discouraging. But perhaps a marriage like that one didn't count. She hadn't really begun to feel like a woman until years after Pangborn floated out of her life, paddling blithely with a swizzle stick down a golden river of highballs. Jack Pangborn, the King of the Golden River, had never been for her. No, that marriage didn't count.

You certainly are a tremendous shrewd picker, she told herself derisively. Your first choice, way back in high school, was a youthful Adonis with an I. Q. of 85 and a dazzling future as a clerk in a chain grocery store. Then there were all those crushes on older men, the men you were going to reform. Finally you followed the dictates of common sense and got yourself romantically involved with an amiable dipsomaniac who half the time couldn't remember your name, and called you Mabel, Gertie, or Flo, as the spirit moved him. When the spirit moved Pangborn beyond your reach and you couldn't go on supporting him for the rest of your life, much as you would have liked to, you nursed a broken heart for years and years. Or was that only a mother complex that got fractured? Whatever it was, you laid off men for a good long time, on account of you had a great sorrow in your life. And meanwhile your salary went up from a hundred to seven fifty a week, because there's nothing like a fractured mother complex, or heart, to fit a girl for making money.

One day you, the shrewd picker, shut both your eyes tight, mumbled a brief invocation to Aphrodite, and reached into the grab-bag again. What came out was Lieutenant Taylor. He looked pretty good for a while, so good that you began to doubt the faultless ineptitude of your own judgment. But all came right in the end when he stood you up in San Francisco and broke your heart, or whatever it was, for good and all. But that wasn't enough. You needed something more to maintain you in the condition of unhappiness to which you had become accustomed. So he married another girl, just to make it permanent. Then he went away into the Pacific and had his ship bombed out from under him and came back and lost his mind. Even that wasn't enough. But the additional things were a little too terrible to think about just now when she was still depressed by the encounter in the hospital. There would be time enough to think about those additional things when she went to see Dr. Klifter.

How on earth did a girl get that way? She'd made a couple of bum choices, but she was no spiritual masochist, in love with a system of diminishing returns, kissing the fists that gave her the old one-two. It was true she'd been tossed out on her ear and had come back asking for more, but that was because he needed her. He needed someone at least, and she had nominated herself. But it wasn't true that she loved him because he needed her. When she'd fallen in love with him for the first and last time, he hadn't needed her at all. She had never met a man more self-contained and independent, and she'd gone ahead and fallen for him just the same. That was back in the fall of '43, when the tide of war was beginning to turn and the only thing that people worried about was winning it. It was really rather pathetic how simple the big things like love and war seemed until you started to go into detail.

She had driven down to La Jolla for the week end —San Diego County seemed to have become the Ithaca of their affair—and had met him at a party there. It wasn't much of a party. Bill and Bella Levy were too careless and informal, and too much in love with each other, to run a really good one. They were content to corral a heterogeneous mob of human beings and turn them loose in the big studio with a radio-phonograph and a case of liquor. Sam Slovell was there that night, and drunk enough to play boogie-woogie on the electric organ.

At one moment she was moving about the room by herself, with a drink in one hand and a cigarette in the other, looking at Bill's abstractionist paintings and Bella's primitives. Male and female created they them, she thought, not much caring which was which. The next moment a young man in Navy blues was moving beside her. He was the only serviceman present, and she'd noticed him earlier in the evening. Without feeling called upon to do anything about it, she'd registered the observation that he looked lonely and out of place. Now he was asking her to dance, and she raised her arms to let him take hold of her. He danced quite well, though he had the look of a man who wouldn't, and she felt pleased with herself because after several hours of moderate drinking she could still dance with a glass in her hand and not spill a drop of her drink.

"You've got a steady hand," he said when the music paused.

She drained her glass and set it down on a table. "Confidentially, I'm controlled by invisible wires."

He laughed dutifully and somewhat unnecessarily. "Let me get you another drink."

"No, thank you. Like half the souses in the world I'm merely a social drinker. But go and get one for yourself."

"I don't drink."

She thought she detected in his tone a trace of provincial self-righteousness which made her want to embarrass him. "But how unusual! I thought all naval personnel simply poured it down."

Instead of blushing he smiled, and she saw with some surprise that he wasn't a dull man at all. "Drinking brings out my paranoiac streak, so I gave it up. My name's Taylor, by the way."

"West is mine." She removed a dried old palette from a bench, and they sat down together. "I take it that when you're inducted into the Navy they take away your first name and give you a number instead?"

"My first name's Bret."

"Mine's Paula."

"I know."

"Really? I thought movie writers were practically anonymous." Damn it, she said immediately to herself, I had to get that in, didn't I? I never can resist a chance to brag.

"I didn't know you were a writer. I asked Bill what your name was an hour ago—as soon as I saw you."

"Why?" From any other woman it would have been a request for flattery, but from her it wasn't. She simply wanted to know.

He took her at her word. "You look honest. I won't deny you've got the trimmings. . . ."

"Did you say your name was Diogenes? Lieutenant (j.g.) Diogenes?" She was flattered after all, but a little irritated too.

"You asked me," he said uncomfortably. "I thought I'd like to talk to an honest woman for a change. I haven't really talked to a woman for over a year."

He was sitting in an awkward and embarrassed attitude with his hands on his knees. His hands were brown and thin, ridged by taut tendons and veins that branched into small blue tributaries, like a contour map of a country she didn't know.

"Does it feel so strange?"

"The whole country seems strange. It strikes you when you come back to civilian society after some sea duty. People seem to be thinking exclusively about themselves."

She thought about the number of bonds she had bought and the number of pints of blood she had given, and wished her record had been better. "Is it different at sea?" she said defensively.

"Maybe not so very different. We have our in-groups and our out-groups. There's a good bit of anti-Semitism, especially among the officers, and of course the Negroes on board get a separate deal. But there's something else besides, an over-all feeling for the ship that comes before everything else. Am I boring the living daylights out of you?"

"No. But I'll bet you're a sociologist in real life."

"Not me. I studied history and law."

"You've been to Washington then."

"I was an underling in the State Department for a while. Does it stick out like a sore thumb?"

"Everybody that goes to Washington comes back so serious-minded."

He answered a little peevishly: "You overestimate me. I always have been serious-minded. I suppose I've gotten worse since we came into the war."

"Were you out long, this last time?"

"Long enough. Just over a year. Nothing to gripe about really. But it makes you feel kind of wooden."

She had noticed that there was something wooden about his face. It was a lean brown mask, as if the pressures of war had forced it into a rigid mold and the Pacific sun had dried and baked it. Each bone and muscle was distinctly anatomized under the tight skin, but the sense of life was to be found only in his eyes.

They were hard and deep, dyed dark blue by the uniform he was wearing.

His eyes were watching the couples still caught and gyrating in the currents of the music. "It's coming back to the States that really gets you down. When you've been out for a while you'd willingly barter your soul for a couple of weeks Stateside. You catch yourself secretly wishing that the engines will break down and you'll have to come back for repairs. As a matter of fact that's what happened."

"You have two weeks?"

"Three weeks. Nineteen days left. But now that I'm here I don't like it."

That had the earmarks of a direct insult, and she could not keep the sharpness out of her voice. "What don't you like?"

"Civilians, I guess. It wasn't so long ago that I was one myself. But now they seem so damn frivolous. There's method in their frivolity of course. They don't forget to look out for number one."

"I take it I strike you as frivolous?"

"Sure you're frivolous. You said you wrote screenplays, didn't you?"

"I try to write as good ones as I can."

"Did you ever write one that wasn't about a couple of nitwits fighting for a permanent possession of a pair of false breasts? Did you ever see one that wasn't?"

"You haven't seen many movies, have you?" She was trying hard to be superior, but she couldn't suppress the anger in her voice. "You probably never heard of *Grand Illusion*, for example?"

"Never did," he admitted cheerfully. "But I've seen enough movies—too many. We have one every night on the ship. Even in the Pacific you can't get away from Hollywood. It covers the globe like a thin coat of paint."

Her reason was beginning to recover and to reflect on the novelty of her position. Like nearly everyone below the rank of producer, she had become hyper-

critical of Hollywood. Griping on the job was the oc-
cupational disease in the writers' building (in the
producers' building it was stomach ulcers). But it was
a little late to tell him that he had taken the words out
of her mouth.

"I suppose you've got to have your daily crack at
Hollywood," she said more coolly. "All intellectuals
do, don't they, like the Boy Scouts and their daily
deed?"

"You don't have to be \an intellectual to get fed up
with general lousiness."

"Of which lousiness I seem to be an integral part?"

"Why reduce everything to the personal?"

"But it's all I can see," she chirped ironically.
"General ideas are terribly bewildering to a frivolous
addlepate like me."

"That griped you, didn't it?" He stood up unexpect-
edly and reached for her hand. "Let's get out of here.
It takes about an hour for boogie-woogie to explore its
limitations."

"You're as opinionative as hell," she said. But she
rose obediently and followed him out of the room.

The concrete steps that led down from the studio
to the shore were steep, and there were a hundred and
fifty of them. Paula was silent as they descended, con-
centrating on her three-inch heels. When they were
part way down she stumbled and took hold of his arm.
She stumbled again before they reached the bottom,
and his muscles tightened in her hand and became as
hard as wood. It gave her a queer feeling, and a rather
frightening one, which her fancy translated into an image of the body beneath the blue uniform, a body
carved by exertion, pared lean by the wind, polished
by the sun, with blankness like a fig leaf guarding her
mind from the bronze loins.

She was glad when the sea spread out before them,
and she let her mind spread with it under the pure
stars. They walked along the dark path toward her hotel. The tide was high and bringing in a heavy surf that

roared lonesomely in the deep coves and struck upon the rocks with white polar paws of foam. It was wild and terrifying to her, like the mating of horses. She shivered a little, though her coat was warm, as if the sea might be able to reach her where she stood.

She couldn't bear to be passively frightened. Deep in her heart she was an animist who believed that the sea was conscious of her and threatening her personally. She stepped over the low wall beside the path, ventured out on a slippery rock just above the reach of the spray, and stood there laughing at the ineffectual waves.

He came up behind her shouting: "You must be crazy! In those heels!"

She turned and laughed at him too. A gust of spray came up and drenched her legs, but she went on laughing.

He put both arms around her and dragged her away from the edge.

"Don't count too much on those invisible wires. You're not drunk, are you?"

"I'm just feeling good. I showed him I wasn't afraid."

"Him?"

"'He,' then, if you must be technical. I showed he!" She laughed in his face.

His embrace was rough and awkward, as if he was performing an unwilling duty, but after years in Hollywood she didn't care for men who were smoothly expert in such matters. She held her face turned up to his to let him kiss her if he wished. When he disregarded the opportunity she felt like a hussy, and her exultation changed to anger.

"You'd better get home and take a hot bath," he said.

"I suppose I'd better."

She hated him warmly all the way back to the hotel. But when, at the last possible minute before they said good night, he asked to see her again next day, she felt unreasonably grateful.

It was a warm day, cloudless and bright, and they went down to the cove in their bathing suits. In any other company Paula would have been the first into the water, but today she didn't need to go in at all. She had a man to take up the challenge for her, a man who put her competitive instinct to sleep. She lay down in the hot sand like any soft little woman, and watched him catch the waves and ride them in. He swam well, and that pleased her. Brains in a man were all very well, indispensable in fact, but you liked a few other things to be added. Broad shoulders, for example, and the ability to swim under water.

The brown man in the waves looked much younger today, younger and freer in the water, as if that other element were his own. He played like a young animal until he was tired and a wave brought him up and stranded him on the beach. He staggered up the slope toward her, breathing hard.

"I bet it's cold."

"Not so cold if you keep moving." He stood on one foot and kicked sideways with the other, shaking the water out of his ears.

"Don't you ever get tired of the sea—after being on it for so long?"

"It depends what sea you're talking about." He sat down in the sand and stretched out beside her. "There are two kinds of sea, and they're as different as day and night. The sea that meets the land, and the sea that's all by itself. Where they come together they sort of kindle each other and make something better than either land or sea. I never get tired of seacoast." He paused and took a long breath. "But when you're in the middle of the ocean and haven't seen anything else for weeks, it's as dull as anything you can think of—a prairie farm, or a boys' prep school in the middle of a desert."

" 'Twas midnight on the ocean,' " she quoted, " 'Not a streetcar was in sight.' "

"Exactly. I get a kick out of looking at the ocean

and not being on it. Not that I see too much of it when
I'm at sea."

"I thought naval officers stood on the bridge in all
weathers, scanning the darkened horizon for enemy
craft."

"The O.D.'s stand on the bridge all right, but we've
never even seen an enemy craft. Our planes do the
scanning for us."

"I didn't know you were on a carrier."

"A jeep carrier. I'm Air Intelligence Officer. My
job is to keep track of the planes."

"Is it hard?"

"It's fairly easy most of the time. But in combat it's
not hard, it's impossible. The instruments aren't perfect yet, and training never is, so every now and then
communications break down. The whole system gets
locomotor ataxia just when we need it most. I won't
try to describe it."

"You sort of have. It must be nice to get home for a
change—" Then she remembered what he had told
her about his disappointment, and quickly added:
"Did you say you had three weeks?"

"Eighteen days now."

"Are you going to stay here?"

"I guess so. I can't think of a better place."

"No folks to go home to?"

"No. Both my parents have been dead for a long
time. Most of my friends are in Washington, but I
don't feel much like going to Washington just now."

She had already, quite shamelessly, begun to plan.
There was no important reason why she shouldn't take
her holiday now. Even if she went ahead and finished
the revision she was working on, her producer was
tied up with other things and wouldn't be ready to go
into production for months. She had been half intend-
ing to spend her holiday in La Jolla anyway. Here,
more than anywhere she knew, land and sea kindled
each other, as he said, and made a new element under
the sun.

He had raised himself on his elbows to look down into her face. "Do you live here?"

"No, but I'm staying here this month."

"I suppose you live in Hollywood?"

"For the last few years I have."

"I wouldn't have thought you were a Hollywood type."

"Hollywood is full of outlandish characters."

"That's not what I mean. You're not outlandish at all."

She smiled up at him. "I'm doing all right."

"I know. I can tell by your clothes. But there are other ways of doing all right."

"What other ways? Kitchen and *Kinder?*"

"Perhaps."

"I tried them."

"*Kinder?*"

"No, no *Kinder.* But I was married for a while. That was a considerable time ago. It didn't work out."

"Oh," he said.

She pressed her advantage. "I did my stint of plain living and high thinking too. I worked for the Detroit *Free Press* for my bread and butter, and wrote for the little magazines for art's sake. Then I met an agent who offered to sell me down the river to Hollywood, and I let him sell me. I was sick of living in a one-room apartment and mending stockings after midnight. Now I just throw them away. Or did before the war."

"Stockings, or dollar bills?"

"*Five*-dollar bills."

That silenced him for a while. "I guess you resent my high moral tone," he said finally.

"I guess I do. I can't help wondering where you got it. You didn't study for the ministry, did you?"

"No." But he added surprisingly: "My father did. He never finished his seminary course though. He lost his faith and turned into a philosophy professor instead of a minister. His religious emotions were transformed into a passion for morality. Morality was an obsession with him, at least after my mother died."

"How old were you when she died?" Already she was becoming infected with a lover's typical symptom and most impossible desire, the desire to share all of his memories, to have known him from the beginning. "Very young?"

"I think I was four. Four or five."

"That's dreadful. What did she die of?"

His face went blank. After a silence he answered: "I don't know."

"But didn't your father tell you?"

"No," he said curtly. "He was a strange man, terribly shy and secretive. I think he should have been a monk."

"What did he look like?" Paula said. "I don't think I would have liked him."

"No. He wouldn't have liked you either. Did you ever see a picture of Matthew Arnold? He looked like him. A long solemn face, intelligent-looking but too heavy, and sort of miserable. He wasn't a happy man."

"You must have been glad to get away from him."

"It wasn't easy. Even after he died I still felt under his thumb. I was at the University of Chicago then, and I tried kicking over the traces, but my heart wasn't in it. That was when I found out I couldn't drink."

"What happened?" she made her question as perfunctory as she could, but she was breathlessly eager to know.

"I got drunk a few times, but I invariably wanted to fight. I had been storing up aggressiveness for fifteen years, and it all came out in the bars. I suppose that's as good a place for aggressiveness as any."

"Aggressiveness against him, you mean? Did you hate your father?"

"I never admitted it to myself, but I suppose I did. For a long time I was afraid even to think anything that he would disapprove of. He never laid a finger on me, but he put the fear of God into me. Of course I loved him, too. Does that sound complicated?"

"Yes, but no more complicated than the way things happen." She thought of her own father, who had been the antithesis of Bret's, an easy-living hard-drinking salesman whose visits home became less and less frequent and finally ceased altogether. She had started out by despising him, but all she felt for his memory now was affectionate tolerance. Tolerance was the most she had felt for anyone for a long time, until now.

A sudden four-o'clock chill drew off the strength of the sun and chased them back to the hotel. But after dinner they came back to the sea again, as if they both secretly recognized that it was the catalyst of their meeting. In the darkness under a palm tree by the public walk he kissed her for the first time, moving toward her with such violent suddenness that she felt waylaid. There was something pathetically arid about his kiss, as if the tropical sun had evaporated his vital juices, and he held her so briefly that she had no time to respond.

The physical inadequacy of his kiss didn't really matter. Already a new element had precipitated from her contact with him in the presence of the sea. The sound of the surf was full of echoes, and the night was larger than it had ever been.

Because he had come from a great distance, from an unimaginable place where planes flew up from carrier decks and combat communications got locomotor ataxia, she had a vivid sense that the ocean stretched far beyond the limit of her vision, curving downward in darkness below the uncertain horizon to military islands and contested waters where the war was being fought. She was invaded by a consciousness that never withdrew again—that she was standing on the edge of a dim infinity from which anything might emerge to meet her: grief, or ecstasy, or death. And she had experienced the three of them.

CHAPTER FOUR

Theodore Klifter watched her as she talked, occasionally stroking his reassuring beard. He had grown this beard involuntarily during a period when he had had no access to shaving materials—it hurt his S.S. guards in their professional feelings when their prospective victims cut their own throats—and he had retained it as a protection for the lower half of his face. The upper half of his face was shielded by thick spectacles that enlarged her image and blurred it slightly, as if there were a wall of glass between them.

The admiration he felt for Paula was not wholly uncritical, though he knew that he made special allowances for tall women who had long brown hair, like the hair his mother had allowed him to brush for her in the evenings when he was a child. Paula was not extraordinarily intelligent, as he preferred women to be, and there was a harsh and irritating contrast between the hard surface of her conversation and the strong vein of emotional femininity in her nature. But she was honest and self-aware. She knew what she wanted and had the stability to wait for it. She was capable of sustaining a grand passion without lapses into moral triviality, and without romantic solemnity. Though other people's lovers were his life's most hackneyed

34

theme, he couldn't help being interested in the man who had won such a love from such a woman.

Her quiet face showed traces of the hard day she had had, but she had plunged into her story as soon as she was seated in his living-room with a drink. He let her talk, for he understood that she had wound up her courage to this point, and was unwilling to give it time to run down.

"You already know, don't you, that he had a severe shock last April when his ship was bombed? It was one of the suicide planes that the Japanese used so much in the last months of the war. A great many of Bret's shipmates were killed, and he himself was rather badly burned and thrown into the water. He was picked up by a crash boat and flown to Guam. He recuperated in the naval hospital there. I didn't know anything about this at the time, but his wife did.

"When he'd been on Guam about four weeks the hospital authorities decided that he was fit to fly home for survivor's leave. His burns were healed, and he showed no signs of a mental condition, at least none appeared in his medical record. He landed at San Francisco after an overnight hop from Hawaii, and after some red tape and delay he caught a train for Los Angeles. He got home about nine thirty at night, but his wife wasn't there."

"Where was she?"

"She was downtown in a bar. The bartender knew her slightly and told the police next day that she had been there. She didn't know when Bret was coming, you see. He couldn't be sure what day he'd catch a plane from Guam, and even if he had, he couldn't have written her on account of the censorship. He should have wired her from San Francisco, but I guess he wanted to surprise her by dropping in out of the blue. Or perhaps he was suspicious of her. Anyway, she wasn't home when he arrived. He was upset and lonely, so he phoned me. I was never so glad to hear from anyone in my life. I didn't care, that night, whether he was married to another woman or not. I picked him up at his house, and we went for a drive."

"How did he behave?"

"Correctly. Too damn correctly."

"That's not exactly what I mean—"

"I know it isn't," she said with a faint smile. "He seemed pretty much as he'd always been except that he was more silent. His manner to me was distant, so much so that I wondered why he'd bothered to call me. He wouldn't talk about his experiences or about the bombing. All I could get out of him was a sort of communiqué. He couldn't conceal his worry about his wife. I drove out Sunset and out the highway toward Malibu, but it wasn't more than an hour before he asked me to take him home again."

"He was eager to see her, then?"

"Yes. I noticed his nervousness, and that may account for it. Of course you'd expect him to be nervous after what he'd gone through. He was thinner than he'd ever been, and he'd never had any excess flesh. He was quite jumpy by the time we got back to his house, and for some reason he asked me to come in with him. I wasn't crazy about the idea of witnessing his meeting with his wife, but he insisted for some reason. I think he wanted to be honest with her, not to deceive her even about a little thing like a car ride. So in I went." She took a long swallow of whisky and soda. The doctor observed that her hand was clenched white around the glass.

"The light was on in the front bedroom—it hadn't been when I called for him—and he opened the door and walked in. I heard him say her name, Lorraine, and then a thud as he collapsed on the floor. I followed him in and saw her lying on the bed naked on top of the bedclothes. She had an enviable figure even in death, but her face was ugly because she had been strangled. I went to the phone and called the police. Then I went back to the bedroom and found that Bret was still unconscious on the floor. I tried to revive him but it didn't do any good. He remained unconscious all night and most of the next day. When the police arrived they found a rolled prophylactic tube on the table beside Lorraine's bed, and other evidence that a man had been with her. The man who murdered her has never been caught."

She was breathing quickly, and the blood had withdrawn from her face, leaving fever spots of rouge on each cheekbone. She raised her glass and finished its contents. "May I have another drink, Dr. Klifter? I didn't realize it would take so much out of me to tell you that." She handed him her empty glass.

When he came back from the kitchen with a strong drink for her and a weaker one for himself, she was standing by the window looking out. Her tailored back was tense and straight in the attitude of listening. Even when she disregarded him she disturbed him, not entirely because she was tall and brown-haired and well made. She was one of the women who without relinquishing their female quality had entered into man's estate. Her body was as streamlined as a projectile, potent as a weapon, but she did not use it to advance her interests or excuse her errors. Europe had had its share of women who lived their own lives and asked for no quarter, but they were the exception rather than the rule. In Los Angeles there were scores of thousands of such women living boldly by their wits, self-contained and energetic atoms in a chaotic society.

He set down the glasses and approached her from behind, looking out through the casement over her broad padded shoulder. She was watching the darkness intently. The walled grounds of the hotel were as quiet and dark as a countryside. The only sound came from a distant bungalow where a radio faintly chided the silence.

With her high heels she was an inch or two taller than he. When they were standing it was hard for him to preserve the patriarchal attitude of his profession. Since he had left his clinic and his professorship and migrated to a strange country, he had found himself dangerously willing at times to slip into a relationship of dependence on such women. He gripped his thick,

dark beard with his right hand and thought earnestly
of himself as a somewhat priestlike figure, superior to
human weaknesses, even his own—a man with
weaned affections, as the American Pilgrims said.

Then she turned to him, and he saw the terror in
her face.

"What is troubling you, Miss West?"

Her voice was shallow and quick, but her whole
body labored to produce it. "I thought I saw somebody outside looking in the window."

"But who?"

"I don't know. Nobody I knew. I only saw two
eyes, or thought I saw them."

"It must have been imaginary. The gates of the
pueblo are locked at eight, and anyone who comes in
must pass the desk. I have never been troubled by
window peepers."

She laughed uncertainly. "Neither have I until lately. But the last few months I've thought there's been
someone following me. Even in my own house I don't
feel safe."

"It's an unsettling experience even if it is not actual."

"Have you had that feeling, Doctor? The sense of
being followed, being watched by malignant eyes?"

She noticed the full highball glass standing on the
coffee table, crossed to it, and drank greedily.

Dr. Klifter looked around the heavily furnished,
anonymous room. For two years he had occupied the
same bungalow in the walled grounds of this pueblo
hotel, but he still considered himself a transient. He
had hung no pictures, bought no furniture, planted no
seeds in the flower beds. The scented stock and early
daffodils bloomed around his house, but they did not
seem to bloom for him. He felt that his only rights
were squatter's right. His trunk was in the closet waiting to be packed. At worst—at very worst—he had
traveler's checks and a volume of Rilke's poems always in his pockets, and was ready to leave at a moment's notice.

"Whenever I leave a doorway," he said, "I look both ways. When I turn a corner I look up and down the street. I know that there is no Gestapo in America, but I have my own Gestapo in my mind. Eventually I hope it may be disbanded. Still my neck is stiff from looking over my shoulder."

"You seem pretty sure that my fears are imaginary." The drink had restored some of the color to her cheeks.

"The things you see, the eyes, and the people that follow you, are almost certainly imaginary. The fears themselves are real. We are all pursued by fears from birth to death, from the fear of being born to the fear of dying. There is no one who has not seen those eyes in the night. I mentioned my own peculiarly Jewish fear as an example."

"You're very kind," she said.

"On the contrary, I am very cruel." He motioned her into a chair and sat down facing her. "But I like to think that mine is the cruelty of a surgeon who amputates in order to save a life. You have been courageous to tell me so much about this murder, and without evasion. Will you tell me one thing more?"

"I will if I can."

"It has occurred to me—I shall be quite as frank with you as you have been with me—that Mr. Taylor's amnesia was, and is, the evasive action of a depleted ego in the face of a guilt that it could not bear. You were with him on that night, and you should be able to clear up that possibility for me."

"Are you asking me whether Bret killed his wife?"

"Yes."

"He didn't. I know he didn't, but you don't have to take my word for it. The police surgeon established that she was killed at about ten thirty, and at that time Bret and I were halfway to Malibu. There was other evidence corroborating the medical testimony. The woman next door heard a scream from the house at that time."

"Was anyone seen to leave?"

"The woman didn't look. She thought the scream was a radio sound effect at the time. Nobody else heard or saw anything till Bret and I found her body."

"The thing is still very vivid to you after nine months."

"Could it help being? I kept the newspaper clippings on the case too. I have them here if you want them."

She rummaged in her bag and produced a wad of clippings held together with paper clips. Unfolding the top layer, she spread it out on the coffee table in front of him. "These are the worst in a way, but the *Examiner* had the most complete coverage."

The doctor glanced rapidly down the columns of print:

There were dark marks of discoloration on her neck, and the face of the dead girl was suffused with blood, according to Dr. Lambert Sims, Assistant Medical Examiner. Dr. Sims quickly established that the young wife had been strangled to death, and criminally attacked as well, scarcely more than half an hour before the receipt of the telephone call from Mrs. Pangborn.

There was ample evidence that a strange man had been present in the room, and the police theory is that the murderer accompanied his victim to her house. None of the other residents of the quiet residential street saw him arrive, or leave after his bloody business was completed. Mrs. Marguerite Schultz, next-door neighbor of the murdered woman, stated at the inquest that she heard a faint scream from the house of death at approximately 10:30 on the night of the murder. Mrs. Schultz testified that she thought nothing of it at the time, attributing it to a crime radio program, but it helped to coroborate the findings of the medical examiner and fix the time of death.

The most sinister and revealing clue was a series of spots of blood on the porch and sidewalk of the murder bungalow. Dr. Sims has been able to establish that these stains were fresh human blood of a different blood-type from that of any of the known principals in the case. But the man who shed that blood, presumed by the police to be the killer, has not yet been apprehended.

Lieutenant Samuel Warren of the Homicide Squad of the Los Angeles police, who is in charge of the case, attaches great importance, also, to a set of fingerprints, evidently those of a man, which were found in the room of horror. These "prints," taken from the surface of the bedside table beside the murder bed, indicate, according to Lieutenant Warren, that the killer leaned upon it in the commission of his foul deed. Eventually, Lieutenant Warren believes, the killer will make the inevitable slip and fall into the clutches of the law. When he does, his fingerprints will be waiting in the police files to convict him.

Dr. Klifter laid down the clipping and drew a long breath. "It is rather hideous, is it not?"

"That's one of the things that reconciles me to Bret's loss of memory. He doesn't have to remember these things. He doesn't even know that his name was in the headlines."

"You've told him nothing?"

"Not I. And fortunately Commander Wright agrees with me. I couldn't bring myself to show him these." She made a gesture of repugnance toward the clippings on the table. "You keep them if you wish. I don't know why I've held on to them so long."

"Thank you. I may have a use for them."

"What use?"

He answered her indirectly: "I'm not sure that the Commander is right—"

"In keeping back these facts? I realize Bret will have to know eventually. But not now. His hold on reality is still so precarious. I don't know what the shock would do to him."

"Nor do I. I hope to understand him better when I have talked to him tomorrow. It may be that the truth of these things, the ugly and naked truth, is exactly what his mind requires. You see, the fact that he is innocent of his wife's death does not exclude the possibility of subjective guilt. It merely removes the most obvious objective reason for his guilt."

"You'll have to take it slower. My brain isn't functioning tonight."

"I shall illustrate my meaning. Suppose that he desired his wife's death. Though he was innocent in all but wish, her death, satisfying as it did his unconscious or partially unconscious desires, might very well leave him with an overpowering sense of guilt. Do you understand me now?"

"Yes," she said in a low voice. "I felt guilty of her death, for that reason."

Her eyes, black with fear, were fixedly watching the dark window again.

PART II

SUNDAY

CHAPTER FIVE

He did his best thinking in the night watches, when darkness and silence swathed his room. Long after midnight he lay awake charging the wilderness of memory that stretched backward from the advancing edge of the present. The motives that explained his life were as difficult to trace as a river that ran underground for more than half its length. But night after night he renewed his groping search. In this dim subterranean place, the hidden life of violence and hatred, tenderness and desire, he might find the self that he had lost, and the key to the door of the room where he lay.

The landmarks of his external life—his boxing championship in college, his graduation *summa cum laude*, his Washington appointment, the publication of his book on the Age of Reason—these things lost all their significance when he looked at them from below, from the vantage point of darkness. The bald ceremony at which he was sworn in as an officer in the Naval Reserve had moved him deeply at the time, but now it was meaningless except as one remote link in the chain of events that had brought him to this hospital bed. His mental crisis, like a crisis in the economy of a nation, had changed the value of his currency.

But there were scenes in his hidden life that seemed

to be lit by a pulsating lightning, a throbbing anguish as secret and intimate as his blood. On his tenth birthday he shot a sparrow with the new air rifle that was his father's birthday present to him. The sparrow flopped crazily around the garden for a long time and refused to die. He had not been able to shoot it again or to touch it with his hands. He stood paralyzed by guilt and repulsion and pity, and watched it beat away its life among the flowers.

Standing by his father's coffin ten years later, he had not been able to grieve. The flower-choked funeral parlor in the little Indiana town bored and irritated him. He was anxious to get back to Chicago and his work. And in the heavy atmosphere of the cut roses and carnations he remembered his tenth birthday. His father had found him with the dying sparrow, and they saw it die together, change in a spasm from a frantic bird to a handful of dusty feathers. They had buried the dead sparrow beside the rosebush, and his father had taken away his air rifle, and he had never seen it again.

He looked down into the rouged and sunken face of Professor Emeritus George Taylor who had sired and fed him, taken away his air rifle, and died unloved in his sleep in his sixty-sixth year. But two days after the funeral he awoke in his Pullman berth on his way back to Chicago and wept for the poor old man and the dead bird. Another ten years had passed since then, but he could still remember the fading eyes of the sparrow as its life went out, and the terrible loneliness of the body in the coffin.

A loneliness as deathly as the dead man's had enclosed him for most of those ten years. He had never been able to take love or give it until he met Paula in La Jolla and she decided to stay with him. Even the day he told her he loved her had been flawed by an impulse of rejection. Though nothing had actually happened and the evil impulse had been rejected in turn, the remembered scene, the moving sky and the gray sea, the dark, sharp cormorants skimming low

over the water, were lit by the guilty lightning in his
mind.

It was the first cloudy day in their week together,
too cold and dark for sun-bathing or swimming in the
cove. A rough wind from offshore reinforced the tide,
and the waves rolled in like hills of glass that shattered
on the deserted beaches. The wind brought color into
her cheeks and made her eyes shine. With a brightly
figured scarf over her hair she was young, absurd, and
lovely, laughing at the white explosions of the waves
bursting on the rocks. They linked hands and climbed
the sea wall as they had on the first night. Threading
their way among the pools and fissures of the water
meadows, they scrambled up on a high rock and stood
there out of reach of the surf.

While they watched the terrific horseplay of the sea,
the seals came in. Usually they stayed a mile or so out,
their raised snouts tiny disappearing cones of darkness
against the shifting colors of the ocean. But sometimes
when their mood was right and the waves were high,
they caught them and rode them in to shore. They
could swim up and out of the crest of a wave, leap
clear, turn in the air, and slide back into their element.
Back and forth they swam inside the breaking rollers,
the continuous grace of their movements as clear to
the watchers as if they were swimming under glass.
Just before the waves swept them to destruction on the
rocks, they ducked and released themselves, swam out
and rode in again. The sleek bodies gliding and twisting in the glass walls were like the bodies of women.
He felt exultant, with an undercurrent of fear and
shame. He had never possessed the body of a woman.

"How I'd love to be a dancer!" Paula said. "To say
things directly with my body, instead of through a
typewriter and actors' faces and camera angles. It
must be the most satisfying art there is."

He didn't answer until the seals had tired, or
thought of another game, and went away. When he
turned to her a tender warmth was trembling through
him.

She faced him gladly, with soft and shining eyes. Her glowing body was hidden like a beast in ambush under her fur coat. He was painfully aware of the warmth of her hand, the whiteness of her chin and throat, the redness of the mouth that was raised to him. His heartbeat was quickened, and his knees loosened by desire. She opened her coat to let him in, and they embraced on the rock above the sea, in full view of two hotels.

It was then that he told her he loved her. But in the dizzy instant of passion the revulsion had taken hold of him. He moved to free himself, but she misinterpreted his movement and held him closer. He felt trapped. She was a divorcee, her kisses were hot and syrupy, her body was cheaply had. She was a woman like the rest. There was no virtue in any of them, as his father had warned him long ago.

He had mastered the impulse, of course, but it had almost overpowered him for a moment: to fling her backward into the boiling surf, let her appetent body be purified and broken. He might so easily have killed her, with a single violent motion have rejected love and lost her forever. Actually he had done nothing to hurt even her feelings. His love for her had drained back into him by way of his head, and he had kept his secret.

It occurred to him now for the first time that perhaps she had not been wholly unaware. They were together for nearly two weeks after that, but they had not become lovers. He had blamed his inexperience and desperate shyness, but it may have been Paula after all who had subtly withdrawn herself. When he asked her to marry him she had preferred to wait. She had seen too many hasty wartime marriages, she said. Of course she wanted to be his wife, but it was better to wait and be sure. When his ship got its sailing orders and headed west again, they weren't even formally engaged.

Still she had been as faithful as a wife, though for nearly a year the only bond between them was the tenuous paper chain of letters. She had written him every day, turning her mind inside out on the pages to show that there was no part of her that didn't love him. His interior life had fed on her letters like an unborn child drawing nourishment through its cords. A letter a day, thirty letters a month. Sometimes when they were on the high seas for weeks at a time, he would hear nothing for a month and reap a harvest of thirty letters at once. The serial number of her letters had mounted to over three hundred when his ship was ordered back to the West Coast to pick up a load of planes.

Security regulations forbade him to tell her in advance, and he had too strict a sense of duty to try to get around them, so that she didn't guess he was coming until he phoned her studio from Alameda. She greeted his voice with incredulous laughter, as if it were a miracle that they should be together on the same continent again. He called her shortly before noon. She caught a plane from Burbank at two o'clock, and a little after four he met her at the San Francisco Airport.

When he saw her tall figure descending the ramp and crossing the apron toward him, he felt a glow of possessive pride that was quickly snuffed out by the fear that he couldn't claim her. From her narrow feet to the tilted hat upon her shining hair she was poised and elegant, moving mysteriously and surely in a female land-world that glittered forever beyond his reach. He saw her through a glaze of time, locked away from him as if in amber.

Then she came through the gate in a little rush, a halting run. Distance and time were annihilated between their bodies. He forgot his doubts and fears, everything but the knowledge of his five senses that he was with her. "It's good to be home," was all he could think of to say against her cheek, and all she could answer was "Yes."

They started out to celebrate in the usual way, drinking at the Top of the Mark, dining at Omar Khayyam's. They talked about the life of ships, which was strange to her, the life of the studios, which was equally strange to him, the life of separated lovers, which they both knew well. But he gradually lost his ability to respond to her intimacy. He was acutely embarrassed by her obvious pride in the double lieutenant's braid that he wore now.

As the hours went by, the hours that he had counted over one by one while he lay sleepless on the last five nights from Pearl, his inner tension increased and became unbearable. Paula sensed his trouble and tried hard to play it down. But after they quarreled at supper her good spirits seemed almost defiant in the face of something that was too much for her but that she'd fight to the last ditch. They both drank heavily, and the midnight taxi-ride to Oakland, which she suggested because she had never crossed the bridge, was a drunken flight from an inescapable reality. Before twelve of them had passed, they knew that their golden hours were being lost.

The final wastage, the jackpot of nothingness, came at the bitter end of the evening. She had managed to sublet a suite in one of the apartment hotels on Nob Hill for the three days they would be together, and she invited him up there for a final drink. From the window of her living-room he could look out over the lighted city like an airman, down the slanted neon streets to the dark harbor, where the ferries and water taxis crossed and recrossed, and the bold arch of the bridge slung across it like a chain of light. His vision was slightly blurred by alcohol, and the whole city stirred like a brilliant armada in a light breeze. A fleet laid out like that would be nice to bomb, he thought. Or a city. A little bombing in the right places would do Frisco a lot of good. Jesus, his head felt rotten! Liquor made him melancholy four times out of five, and the fifth time it made him wild. It seemed to affect Paula hardly at all except to heighten her reactions, and that was all she understood about it.

She came up quietly behind him and closed her arms around his waist. "It's beautiful, isn't it?" she

said. "Greater than Troy or Carthage. There are three
cities in this country that give me the feeling of great-
ness, the feeling I had when I went to London and
Paris. New York, Chicago, and San Francisco. That
sounds like the name of a railway, doesn't it? A su-
per-railway with no changeover at Chicago."

"There's nothing left of Troy," he answered som-
berly, "and they sowed salt on the ruins of Carthage."

She laughed softly in his ear. "You and your tragic
sense of history! I wasn't thinking of anything like
that. They have a romantic sound to me, is all. And
they were big navy towns in their day."

He resented her laughter, her easy rejection of his
mood. To his whisky-sickened nostrils the perfume in
her hair was overpoweringly sweet. He resented her
material perfection, the long polished nails of the
hands that held him, the fine clothes he could not have
bought for her, the lofty rooms he could not have rent-
ed. They had quarreled at supper when she had tried
to pick up the check. Though she had seen her error
and given in immediately, his humiliation still rankled.

"You're a very independent woman, aren't you?"
he said.

She was silent for a moment, then answered mat-
ter-of-factly: "I suppose I am. I've been on my own
for a good many years." But her embrace slackened,
and she drew back from him a little as if in self-de-
fense. "You wouldn't want me to be a clinging vine,
would you?"

He laughed harshly. "There's not much danger of
that." He was still facing the window. The lights of the
city outside were bright and heartless, like cruel eyes.
San Francisco, the city he had dreamed of for a year,
meant no more to him now than the empty camouflage
cities built to mislead enemy bombers.

"I thought you liked me as I was, Bret. I'm sorry if
I did the wrong thing at supper. I've simply gotten into
the habit of paying my way. It's a measure of self-pro-
tection in Hollywood."

He stirred angrily, and her hands fell away from

him entirely as he turned to face her. "I don't know much about your Hollywood crowd, but that seems like a funny attitude to take to me. I thought we were going to be married—"

"We are."

"What sort of place will I have in your life if I'm your husband?"

"What are you trying to do? You're making a difficulty where none exists."

"On the contrary. The difficulty may be insuperable."

"Listen to me," she said. "I don't even know what we're quarreling about. Those weeks in La Jolla I thought I learned to understand you. Whether I did or not, you took reality with you when you went away. All the time you were out my life here seemed unreal. Before I met you it was the war that was unreal, but since then it's all I've cared about."

He had hurt her once, and the resulting pain made him strike out blindly again. "No doubt I've given you some very authentic touches for your next war picture."

She threw away her vanity and took hold of his unbending body. "Don't be a bastard, darling. You can't be jealous of my work."

"That's a laughable thought."

"Then what's the matter? I was crazy with happiness when you phoned this morning. I thought everything would be wonderful, and it hasn't been. Don't you love me?"

He answered with an effort: "I don't know."

"All your letters said you loved me. Have I done something to spoil it? Turn around and face me."

He turned in the circle of her arms and looked down into her face. There was a spillage of tears from the corners of her eyes, which she tried to blink away. She closed her eyes and leaned toward him.

"I know you love me," said her red and swollen mouth. "Forget whatever it is, Bret. Just love me."

He lacked the power to accept her love. His mind

went whimpering backward down the past to stand transfixed by a dead face on a pillow. He was as cold as the face of his dead mother; his heart perished in her mortmain grip. He took Paula by the shoulders and pushed her away from him.

Her face was torn by grief and anger, but she kept her voice steady. "I don't know what the matter is, Bret, but you'd better go now."

"I suppose I'd better."

"You'll call me tomorrow?"

"I don't know. Good night. I'm sorry."

He heard her crying softly while he waited in the funereal hallway for the elevator. The dead hand of the past held him by the arm, and the image of the dead woman descended with him in the automatic elevator and followed him out into the slanting street.

Lying in his hospital bed a year and a half later, he could see his mother's face as clearly as he had then: the marble face of the long dead, closed to the sight, unresponsive to the touch, with hair like wings of darkness folded on the brow. She had died when he was four, more than twenty-five years ago, but the image of her face hung on the wall of every room he entered, and the cold memory of her death still chilled him to the bone. Yet so far as he could remember, she had died naturally in bed. The trouble was that he didn't remember very well. His brain was a whispering gallery thronged with uncertain images.

His memory of what he had done after he left Paula was doubly confused because he had gone on drinking the next day. He knew nothing else about it, but he could taste the whisky in the passages between his nose and throat and recall the buzzing alcoholic emptiness of his head. He had gone down in the automatic elevator, crossed the steep street to a taxi stand, and disappeared from his own consciousness.

A few months before, he had been willing enough to forget, but now he was fiercely impatient with his lagging mind. His memory was perfectly good for the unimportant things. He knew the names of Napoleon's marshals, the call signs of the ships they had operated with off Leyte, his telephone number in Arlington, his street address in Los Angeles. No, not Los Angeles. He had never lived in Los Angeles. That was a queer sort of slip to make, and he was always making them. Parapraxis, the doctors called it, and said it was perfectly normal, but he was not consoled. It was terrifying not to be able to trust your memory.

Still, he was getting better. Nine months ago he had been utterly lost in time and space. Now he knew who he was, where he was, why he was here. He repeated the facts like a consoling liturgy. Bret Taylor, Lieutenant, USNR, Naval Hospital, Eleventh Naval District, San Diego. Forgetfulness. The day was Saturday. Sunday, rather, since it was past midnight. Sunday, February 24, 1946. Not 1945, but 1946, and the war was over. It had taken him a long time to catch on to that, but once he got hold of a thing he never let go of it. The problem was to get hold of those lost days in Frisco. All he had was the whisky taste, the buzzing emptiness, and the sense of disaster. Something disastrous had happened, but he did not know what it was. Paula might have told him, but he had been ashamed to ask her.

Whatever had happened, she had stuck by him. A year and a half later she was still coming to see him every week. She wasn't married to him as he had imagined, but she was standing by. The thought of her was an island of security among the uncertainties of his mind. He went to sleep with the thought of her standing by his bed. But it was not Paula he dreamed of.

CHAPTER SIX

He awoke at his usual time, with the taste of the dream in his mouth and a name on his lips waiting to be spoken. The dream faded quickly when he opened his eyes, but he remembered a multitude of bars telescoping into a dreary penny arcade flavored with whisky. In one of the games of chance he had won a kewpie doll with bright blue eyes. It sat on his shoulders like an old man of the sea. He didn't want the doll on his shoulders, but he had won her in the arcade and she was his responsibility. A policeman with a face like Matthew Arnold proclaimed the fateful words: "Be ye married to disaster until death do us part." The Matthew Arnold face withered away to a skull, and the kewpie doll danced on his grave in Alsace-Lorraine.

"Lorraine," his dry lips repeated. He was married to a girl named Lorraine. But only yesterday Paula had told him that he had no wife.

He put on his bathrobe and slippers, and ran down the hall to Wright's sleeping quarters. There was no answer to his knock. He tried the door and found that it was locked. He knocked again.

A hospital corpsman came round the corner from

the duty desk. "The commander isn't here, Mr. Taylor. Is there something you want?"

"Where is he?"

"He went up to L.A. last night. Lieutenant Weising's on duty."

Weising wouldn't do. He was too young, and he couldn't talk freely to Weising. "I want to talk to Commander Wright."

"He said he'd be back sometime this morning. Can it wait?"

"I suppose it'll have to."

But his mind wouldn't wait. After a breakfast that he was unable to eat, he went back to his room to continue his reconstruction of the past. The dream of the kewpie doll, and the single name it had deposited in his mind, filled him with acute anxiety. But it was the clue he needed, the Ariadne thread in the San Francisco labyrinth.

It took him to a room he remembered very clearly: every detail of the peeling walls, the cracked blind, the clouded mirror hanging precariously over the bureau. He had found this room in a cheap hotel after he left Paula, and had spent a bad night on the thin edge of sleep. He managed to sleep for a couple of hours in the morning, but that was all. Some time before noon he went out and bought a bottle of whisky. He drank a few shots by himself in his room, but the alcohol only depressed him, and he was gripped by loneliness. Company was what he needed, any sort of company. He hid the bottle on the top shelf of the closet and went out to look for a bar.

There was a bar where the singing waiters wore handlebar mustaches and served beer in foaming mugs. There was a bar whose walls and ceiling were mirrors reflecting a sickly fluorescent light and women's waiting faces. There was a bar with naked pink ladies painted on the walls, their nipples as large and red as maraschino cherries. There was a bar with a roughly finished interior like a log cabin, and a basement where submarine men could play at being under water. He felt out of things there and went to other bars. There was the place in Chinatown where a girl in a kimono served him fried prawns and he was sick in his booth. He had never before drunk past the first onset of drowsiness and sickness, but that day he did. There was a long series of bars, indistinguishable from each other, with a jukebox at one end and a pinball machine at the other. In each of them a white-jacketed bartender with a bored and knowing face served drinks in a semidarkness to shadowy couples and single men and women hunched on leather stools. In one of these, behind the smoke screen of noise that the jukebox laid, the nightmare of Lorraine had begun.

The scene he remembered had the earmarks of a dream. There were a number of people in the long room, but none of them made a sound. His own voice, competing effortlessly with the brawling of the jukebox, issued from his throat without moving his lips. His legs and feet, the hand with which he paid for their drinks and raised his glass to his mouth, seemed as remote as Pacific islands. But he felt carefree and powerful, borne up and thrust forward like a plane by the buzzing in his head.

Of course it hadn't been a dream. Lorraine had been a real girl sitting not in some cavern of the unconscious, but in an actual bar drinking genuine whisky. For a girl of her age she seemed to have a remarkable capacity. If the truth were known she probably had no right to be drinking in a bar at all. They were strict with minors in California, and she didn't look twenty-one. Her face was extraordinarily innocent, he thought, and extraordinarily sweet. The whiteness of her low, broad forehead was marbled with delicate blue veins and framed in black hair. Her long brows, which had not been plucked artificially thin like Paula's, gave her blue eyes a pure and steadfast look. Yet there was nothing heavy about her face. Her short upper lip, repeating the upward tilt of her nose, gave it an impish gaiety accentuated by her full, impulsive mouth. She looked like an innocent kid from out of town who had blundered into a dive by mistake and was quite untouched by her surroundings.

He felt a certain responsibility for her, as he felt responsible for all weak or innocent or helpless people. It was only natural that he offered to buy her a drink.

"I don't mind if I do," she said. "Two stripes mean a full lieutenant, don't they?"

"Yes," he said. "I like your face. You have a lovely, pure face."

She wriggled and giggled. "You Navy boys are fast workers. Been out a long time?"

"Nearly a year this last time." He leaned toward the fragrance of her hair, which was sleek and heavy on her shoulders. When he inclined his head, his mind descended in a dizzy spiral round and round her body like a wreath. He said in a choked whisper: "I like the way your hair smells."

She laughed with pleasure and turned her head quickly back and forth so that her hair flew out against his face. "You ought to. That's expensive scent. What's your name, sailor?"

"Bret."

"That's a nice name, so unusual. Mine's Lorraine."

"I think Lorraine is a beautiful name," he said.

"You flatter me."

He seized her hand and kissed its moist palm. The bartender gave him a brief, cynical glance.

"Be careful, Bret. You'll spill our drinks."

"To hell with them! I've got a quart of Harwood's in my room. This stuff makes my throat dry anyway."

"I like Harwood's," she said with girlish candor.

"Let's go then."

"If you want to, Bret dear."

She slid off the stool and buttoned her coat. She was surprisingly small, but her figure had the dignity of perfection. As she moved ahead of him to the door he saw how the hips under the tight coat bloomed out from the narrow waist, swaying with every tap of her quick heels. His mind swayed with her body, and his eyes undressed her.

Twenty minutes later he undressed her with his hands. The taxi ride to his hotel had been a continuous kiss, and he was breathless and dizzy. She let out her breath to help him with a last difficult hook and eye and lay back smiling. He was amazed by her body's economy and richness. Beneath the luxury of her breasts he could feel the fragile ribs. He could span her waist with his hands. But the sweep of her hips was terrifying, and the blandness of her belly and thighs, and the panther blackness of her hair.

When he turned out the light the whole night became panther-black and terrifying and sweet. Her kisses were the fulfillment of a promise too sweet to be believed, like a springtime in midwinter. Somewhere inside him the ice went out with a rush. The black night flowed like a river toward the delectable mountains, through a narrow, desperate gorge, into a warm valley where eventually he went to sleep.

This time Commander Wright was in his office and called to him through the open door to come in.

"Do you mind waiting a minute, Taylor? I should have got this stuff out yesterday." He was working at his desk on a typewritten report, emending it with a red pencil that threatened to snap under the pressure of his thick fingers.

Bret sat down in a hard chair to wait. His body was tense with anxiety. Unless he was having delusions again he had done the one thing that fouled up his life completely. He remembered waking up in the morning with the girl in bed beside him. His head rang like a cracked bell, but a drink from the dwindling bottle of Harwood's softened its tone. He went back to the sleeping girl and was fascinated again by her half-covered body shining in the dingy room. He had wakened her with his hands, and she turned toward him as soft and sensuous as a kitten. All this had been bad enough for a man of his moral pretensions (and the

day after Paula had flown five hundred miles to be
with him), but it wasn't the chief thing that was
worrying him now. He seemed to recall that when they
ran out of whisky and went out to buy more, he also
bought a marriage license.

"Bloody Navy red-tape," Wright grumbled. He
looked up from his papers and retrieved his dead pipe
from the ashtray. "I suppose you came to get the word
on Dr. Klifter? Well, he's here. He drove down with
me this morning."

"I don't understand, sir."

"Didn't Miss West tell you he was coming?"

"No, sir."

"He's a friend of hers, a well-known psychoanalyst.
He was one of the original members of the Viennese
Society until he broke with Freud. Then he ran his
own clinic in Prague before the war. He's been prac-
ticing in L.A. the last few years."

"Very interesting," Bret said. "But how do I come
into all this?"

"He came here to interview you, I thought you
knew. He's going over the files with Weising now. If
he thinks your case is susceptible to psychoanalytic
treatment, we'll arrange for it—"

"Who's going to pay for it? I can't afford the luxury
of a psychoanalyst from Middle Europe."

"Miss West is handling that."

"I see."

"You don't seem very pleased. If he takes the case
you'll get a leave out of it. Don't count on it, but that's
what's in the book."

"I've given up counting on anything." Under different circumstances the prospect of a leave would have
delighted him. But all he could think of right now was
the stranger he had slept with, or married. If he had
married her it meant the end of the one thing he cared
about. When Paula found out, if she didn't already
know. . . . But she must know. Why hadn't she told
him?

Wright gave him a narrow look. "Is there something bothering you, Taylor?"

"Yes. Am I married? I know how irresponsible that sounds."

Wright's nostrils emitted twin streams of smoke like a benevolent dragon's. "Close the door, will you? Thanks. Now sit down."

"Do you have a record of a girl called Lorraine? It's important to me to know—"

"Yes. You plan to marry Miss West, don't you?"

"Answer my question," Bret said sharply. "I don't see any reason for making a mystery of it."

"I'm not making a mystery out of it, Taylor. Your own mind did that."

"All right, all right. Am I married?"

Wright knocked out his pipe as if extinguishing an impulse to ease his patient's tension. "You can't go on using my memory indefinitely. You're getting to be quite a big boy now."

"Yes, sir," Bret said in flat hostility.

"Let's see, you met this Lorraine Berker in San Francisco in the fall of '44. Can you tell me about her? What she looked like?"

"She was a blue-eyed brunette, a very pretty girl." He adopted the doctor's past tense with a half-unconscious recognition of its aptness. "She had a remarkably white skin for a brunette."

"Is that the way she looked the last time you saw her?"

"I don't know. I'm trying to think." He caught a glimpse of Lorraine's face stained with sleep and tears as it had been the morning he left her. The ship was due to weigh anchor at eight, and he had to leave the hotel at five to allow time for the long ride to Alameda. He had kissed her for the last time, on mouth and eyes and breast, and left her in what must have been their marriage bed. "I married her, didn't I? Before I sailed? Is it in the record?"

Wright permitted himself to say yes.

"Where is she now?"

"Remember for yourself, man."

Another face in another bed (the old spool bed his father had bought in Boston?) came over the horizon of his conscious mind and into memory's middle distance. It wasn't Lorraine. Yet he couldn't be sure. Death did strange things to people's faces.

"Is she dead?" he whispered.

"You tell me." Wright's predatory eyes were stalking him from the underbrush of his eyebrows.

"I remember a dead woman. She had on a black silk dress."

"Your mother," Wright said irritably. "That all came out in narcosynthesis, remember? She died when you were very young."

"My sense of chronology seems to be a little scrambled." And this fat-faced doctor, arrogant and smug like every man with too much gold braid on his sleeve, wasn't giving him any help. He sat behind his desk as bland as a Buddha, with all the important secrets locked in his thick skull.

Instead of the truth he had asked for, Wright was making him listen to a talk on elementary metapsychology: "Time is a relative concept," he was saying. "The mind is like a clock with several faces, each keeping its own time. One for the minutes and hours, one for the seasons and the years, one for the individual biological development, one for the mental life, and so on. On the level of motivation and emotional reaction the mind is practically timeless. Freudians like Klifter say that the clock is set once in early childhood and never changes unless you go back and give the hands a push. I think that's an oversimplification, but there's a good deal of truth in it. Klifter said on the way down that you're probably identifying your wife and your mother, though they died over twenty years apart."

"Then Lorraine is dead?"

"You know she is, don't you?"

"How did she die?"

"You've got to remember for yourself. Klifter may have different ideas, but so long as I'm handling the case it's going to be that way. It's our only guarantee against a relapse. I could tell your conscious mind, but it wasn't your conscious mind that wiped out the memory. The unconscious levels have to accept the fact. The only way you can demonstrate that they have is by recovering the memory yourself."

"I can't see any purpose in this mystification."

Wright shrugged heavily, like a man shifting a weight on his shoulders. "It would be nice and easy to overhelp you, but I'm not going to do it. You're going to stand on your own feet, understand?" He got to his feet as if to emphasize the metaphor.

Bret rose at the same time, but Wright waved him back into his chair. The gesture, in combination with his dark blue uniform, accentuated his resemblance to a burly policeman. "You might as well wait here. I'll go and see if Klifter's ready for you."

Bret sat down to wait again. His resentment died down suddenly as soon as Wright had closed the door behind him, and depression took its place. In the space of a few hours he had been married to an unknown girl and widowed in an unknown way. It seemed to him that time was the meaning of his life, and he had lost it. His future was still in the inescapable past, and he was caught in a closed circle as meaningless as the treadmill in a rat cage and as timeless as hell.

CHAPTER SEVEN

Externally Bret seemed to be a typical young American, big, smooth-faced, and brown, with a strongly constructed nose and chin, and candid blue eyes. The only sign of inner disturbance that Klifter noticed in the first few minutes came when the young man's eyes roved to the window. Then the heavy muscles of his shoulders bunched and strained under his gray fatigue uniform, as if the narrow office hemmed him in and he was held in his low steel chair by an invisible belt. When he withdrew his eyes from the green vista of the hospital grounds, his face had taken on a complexity that had not been apparent at first.

The eyes were not blue after all, but blue flecked with gray. The combination of color gave them depth and modified their transparency. They seemed to contain more than one surface, like a series of lenses that filtered and selected their perceptions before they reached the brain. The mouth was equally complex, the generous softness of its natural molding held in a firm line by an aggressive will. The conflicts in the young man's nature, of which he seemed intelligently aware, gave him a kind of tense, self-conscious beauty. But Klifter was disturbed by the ironic bitterness that when he smiled cast a shadow in his eyes and deformed his mouth.

The newspaper clippings Paula had given him the night before were in the inside pocket of his coat. If Taylor's mind was moving toward reality and health, a full knowledge of the event that had alienated him from these things would help him on his way. But if his mind was seriously ill, caught in the grip of a psychotic perversity, the knowledge of the murder might strengthen his disease. Truth was a potent drug that could kill or cure, depending on the patient's stomach for it. His problem, as always, was to understand the individual man.

He turned to Bret, who was silent in his chair, emptily gazing at the floor.

"Please go on. I should like to learn more of your childhood life."

Bret stirred uneasily. "From the beginning?"

"Not necessarily. I do not attach the importance which Adler does to the earliest memories. I am more interested in what you consciously think important."

"My attitude, you mean?"

"Give me the facts. Your attitude has been speaking for itself."

After some embarrassed hesitation Bret resumed his interrupted narrative.

"You must have gathered that my home life when I was a kid was pretty queer. I don't think it was before my mother died, but she died when I was four so I don't remember much about that. My father's older sister came to keep house for him, and for a couple of years I was under her thumb. Aunt Alice, or perhaps it was my father, set up some rather peculiar rules for a five-year-old to live by. I remember she spanked me on at least one occasion for asking questions about my mother. She wouldn't even tell me what had happened to her. Aunt Alice died herself when I was six, and I can't say I was sorry." He smiled his disturbing smile again, tightening his mouth as if these memories had a bitter taste.

"That's natural enough," Klifter said. "The stern old aunt would make a poor substitute for your dead mother. Who looked after you when the aunt died?"

"My father took care of me himself. He was a full professor at that time, and vice chairman of his department, and he could have afforded a nursemaid. But for some reason he wouldn't have a woman in the house. He went to an inordinate lot of trouble with me, and probably slowed up his own work considerably, simply in order to avoid living with a woman. He hired male students of his, off and on, to help with the cooking and the cleaning, but he and I did most of the housework ourselves. I could cook quite well when I was eight, but I didn't learn to play baseball until I went to prep school. He only let me stay in prep school for one term, by the way. All of which probably accounts for my inability to fit into a group, my feeling that I have no definite place in society."

"Yes, probably."

"When I look back on it I can see that I've been a good deal of a lone wolf all my life. Even my profession—I don't believe I told you I write history, or used to—was a one-man sort of thing. I never did much in team games, but I was good at boxing and swimming. The only thing I ever got into where I felt carried away by something greater than myself was the Navy. After I was given my commission, and especially when I was assigned to my ship, I felt for the first time in my life that I belonged to something. I was a member of a team fighting for a good cause, and it gave me a satisfaction I'd never had. I turned out to be a pretty good officer, curiously enough. I got along well with my men and did my job. When the ship went down I had a sense of irreplaceable loss."

"You were—invalided out, I believe, before the war ended?"

"Yes. I think I know what you're driving at. I've gone into it rather thoroughly with Commander Wright. It's true I felt guilty about dropping out of the fight before it was finished. It's also true that I didn't want to go back after my ship was bombed. I was completely tired out after more than two years at sea, and I guess I was frightened too. I didn't admit it then, even to myself, but I do now."

"What exactly do you admit?"

Bret withdrew his eyes from Klifter's and looked away out of the window again. His hands strained against the arms of his chair as if it were a trap. "I admitted to Commander Wright, and to myself, that I was secretly glad when my ship went down. It meant survivor's leave for me." His voice cracked on the final word.

"I see. You are still suffering from a sense of guilt?"

"Maybe I am," Taylor said impatiently. "But it has nothing to do with that."

"I think it has. You cannot yet live comfortably with the knowledge of your own weakness. Remember that it is a normal human weakness to value self above all others. I have harbored a similar wish, Mr. Taylor. When the candidates were selected for the crematorium each day, I silently prayed that I would not be one of them, though there were many others less fit to die. We all must learn to live with the dreadful fact of our own selfishness. There is no virtue in futile guilt."

"That's what Wright said, and I believe it. Some of these dreadful facts take a lot of getting used to, that's all. But it isn't that that's bothering me now."

"What is bothering you now?"

"The things I can't remember," he said in a dry, wretched voice. Suddenly he blurted: "Doctor, what happened to my mother?"

"Your mother?"

His smile was equally wretched. "Did I say 'mother'? I meant to say 'wife.' I meant to ask you what happened to my wife. I didn't even know I had a wife until today."

"She is dead. I am sorry." Klifter spread his hands in a gesture of embarrassment and sympathy.

"But how did she die?"

Klifter had not yet made his decision, and he took refuge in a Jesuitical half-truth: "I do not know exactly. Tell me about your mother, Mr. Taylor. Do you remember her?"

"Yes." After a long pause he added: "She was quite a pretty woman. I remember that much, but she's rather vague. I told you she died when I was four. She was good to me. I had fun with her. She used to stand on her head on the bed for me, things like that. We had pillow fights. And we had a game at meals, about my eating. One bite for each of her ten fingers, or something. She had lovely hands."

"Do you remember her death?"

The dreaming blue eyes hardened in rejection. "No. Wait a minute—I remember something." His eyes glazed and lost their focus. His brown face became smooth and blank, a wooden image of a young boy set out to decoy the past. "I went into her room, and she was dead. Some nights when I was afraid, she would let me come into her bed and stay until I was asleep. I had a bad dream that night and went into her room, and she was stiff and cold. I could see her dead face in the light from the head of the bed. Her hands were folded on her breast. I touched her face, and it was as cold as a wet cloth."

"Was she wearing her nightgown?" Klifter recalled that Lorraine had been naked when Taylor found her.

"No." The answer was very definite. "She was wearing a black silk dress with a white ruffle at the throat. Her eyes were closed, and her head was resting on a white satin pillow. I didn't know that she was dead until my father told me. I had never seen a dead person before."

"Did your mother usually sleep on a white satin pillow?"

"What do you mean? How do you expect me to remember a thing like that? My mother died when I was four."

Klifter refrained from pointing out that Taylor had recalled the detail himself. Because this line of inquiry seemed to be disturbing to the young man, he abandoned it for the moment.

"Tell me, was your mother's death a frequent memory, or a painful one?"

"In my childhood, you mean?"

"Yes."

"I didn't often think of my mother at all. One reason must have been that my father never mentioned her. I think he may have grieved for her in private. Certainly he wasn't a happy man and he never remarried, but so far as I remember he didn't talk about her. He wouldn't even answer my questions about her, and he discouraged my asking them. He let me understand that the subject was taboo. Naturally I got the impression that there was something wrong there, but I never dared to ask him what it was."

"Perhaps he did not love your mother?"

"Perhaps he didn't. The thought wouldn't have occurred to me when I was a kid, but it has since. I told you how he felt about women in general. He brought me up to regard them as whited sepulchers, lovely receptacles of the world's filth—that sounds like exaggeration, but it isn't. So long as I was at home, and I was with him up to the age of seventeen except for my term at prep school, I wasn't allowed to have anything to do with girls. He wouldn't let me buy a girl a soda or go to a mixed party. I didn't go out with a girl until after his death—I was in my senior year at Chicago —and then nothing came of it. I was a virgin until my marriage." He corrected himself hastily. "The night before my marriage."

Paula West? the doctor wondered. Surely she would have told me. But perhaps not. Every woman has her reticences, like every man.

Bret understood the silence and answered the unspoken question. "I slept with my wife the night before I married her. It's a curious thing," he added hesitantly. "I dreamt about it this morning." He told Klifter what he could recall of the kewpie-doll dream.

"I suppose it means I married Lorraine under the influence of my father's morality?"

"Or slept with her as a gesture of revolt against him? A dream may have multiple meanings. We will talk about your dream at another time."

Klifter rose from his chair and moved impatiently about the small office. While great areas of the biography were blurred or missing altogether, the patterns of Bret's mental life had begun to configure in his mind. There was clearly a fixation on the death of the mother for which the father's foolish treatment of his son seemed partly responsible. But the evidence of it had come too easily, almost without resistance. The very readiness and clarity of the infantile memory made it suspect, especially in view of the similarity between the death of the mother and the death of the wife. It was clearly possible that the mother's death scene was a substitute, elaborately staged by the analysand's imagination, for the inadmissable memory of the murdered wife. This possibility was strengthened by the evident identification of the mother and the wife, whom Bret had confused verbally. The pattern was OEdipean, complicated by a melancholia arising from what Bret described as his sense of loss. He had lost his mother at a vulnerable age, lost his ship and the comradeship it symbolized, lost his wife. He was one of those who had formed the habit of loss and acquired a need for it, especially where his affections were concerned. He had done his best to lose Paula West. Finally he had lost his memory and for a while reality itself.

Commander Wright believed that the truth Bret had lost should be withheld until Bret found it himself. Like many American doctors, even some who had learned from Freud, Wright was basically a moralist. He believed that mental disease was an evasion of responsibility by the patient, and that it was therefore a doctor's duty to his patients to let them cure themselves so far as possible. Heaven helped those who helped themselves.

But it was possible that the motives behind Wright's muscular attitude were not entirely moral. Klifter had noticed during their conversation on the road that Wright was deeply interested in Paula West. This sexual interest in his patient's lover might have influenced him to take the longest way in his treatment of the case, avoiding the drastic shortcut on which Klifter had decided. There was also the fact that Paula was opposed to Bret's being told the truth, and Wright took her opinions very seriously.

Wearily he dismissed the elaborate train of conjecture. The case must be judged on its merits rather than on the basis of hypothetical motives of the other people involved. The only question to be decided was Taylor's relation to the blurred and wavering line that separated the sheep from the goats, and his mind was already made up.

His hand was in his pocket palpating the wad of clippings when he was overcome by caution. What if he made his potent gift of truth and Taylor then refused to become his patient? The results could be embarrassing, not to say disastrous. He must be certain before he prescribed this medicine that the case was his.

"Do you wish to see me again?" he said. "Do you think I can help you?"

"I'd like to think so. I'd grab at anything that promised to pull me out of this backwater. If I don't get back to work soon I'll lose the habit permanently."

"What work are you planning? It is good for you to be thinking of going back to work."

"It's a book I've had in mind for a long time. I call it *The Political Fallacy*. It's nothing startlingly original, the idea goes back away before Thoreau, but I want to make some modern applications of it. The leading fallacy of our times, underlying fascism and communism and even most of the liberalisms, is the belief that political man is man in his highest function, that political forms are the salvation of the individual soul— But don't let me bore you," he concluded miserably.

"On the contrary. Please go on. I take it you are no anarchist?"

"Call me a political protestant. Your true anarchist is the enemy of political forms of any kind. I simply want government to know its place. A state, or a political party, is a means to an end. The end has got to be determined by non-political values, or politics becomes a snake gagging on its own tail. You have an analogous problem in psychiatry, don't you? Whether to prepare your patients for the absolutely good life or for the life of society. That's a crude antithesis, but you know what I mean."

"I do indeed. That is one of our basic problems. Especially in a period when the good life and the life of society may be at opposite poles. In an insane society it is the sane man who seems insane."

"I can't take that comfort to myself," Taylor said with his bitter smile.

"You have no reason to despair. The final test is ability to work, and your mind displays great energy."

"And produces nothing. You can hardly imagine how unsettling it is not to remember certain things. It's as if my own back yard were full of hidden land mines. I know I planted them myself, but I can't remember where."

"You know as well as I that every man has within him, in his back yard as you say, the total range of good and evil. But nothing there is less than human. You will find that nothing there can blow you to pieces."

"Then what happened to my wife?" Taylor's voice had suddenly become violent and high. "Why has nobody told me?"

"Consider that you did not know you had a wife until today. Commander Wright has allowed your process of recall to follow a natural course."

Taylor twisted in his chair in order to look up into Klifter's face. "I can't live in a cage for the rest of my life. I feel as if they've shut me away in a drawer in a mausoleum."

"I understand your feeling," Klifter said quietly. "Shall we meet again then?"

"If you think it will do any good. Commander Wright said something about a leave."

"Yes. If you come to stay with Miss West in Los Angeles you will be accessible to me. She has already taken it up with Commander Wright's superiors. You will come to see me this week in Los Angeles then?"

"I have no choice, have I?"

"Your choices are voluntary. You are legally a free man—"

"I didn't mean to be ungrateful," Taylor said. "If I had a choice, or since I have, I'll come."

"Good. In the meantime it will be well for you to read these." He brought the wad of clippings out of his pocket and handed them to Taylor. "We will talk of them at our next meeting."

The young man stared at them. "What are they?"

"The newspaper accounts of your wife's death. She was murdered nine months ago. Your illness had its inception at that time."

Bret had sprung to his feet and was standing over the doctor, his irises shining grayly like small spinning wheels. "Who killed her?"

"The murderer is unidentified and still at large. When you have read those articles you will know all that I know."

"I see now what the mystery was," Taylor said slowly. "The bloody fools!"

"You must excuse me now," Klifter said. "Goodbye. I should say au revoir." The German phrase had risen to his lips, but he suppressed it, as he tried to suppress all German things to himself.

Bret was so absorbed in the newsprint in his hands that he failed to answer. With a last look at his tormented face Klifter went to the door. Superficially, he reflected as he closed it behind him, these Americans were an optimistic and secular brood. Incessant radios routed their loneliness, five-color advertisements and chromium bathrooms exorcised their diseases, mortuaries like the mansions of heaven disguised their funerals. But the tragic inner life went on, strong in proportion to its denial and violent in proportion to its stealth. The handsome barbered heads and sun-tanned faces were shadowed by death. Even more than the others, it seemed to him, Taylor had been engaged in a lifelong struggle with death. Let him meet his adversary face to face.

PART III

MONDAY

CHAPTER EIGHT

The afternoon was warm for February, and they drove with the top down. It was good to be on the road again after the last dragging hour at the hospital, packing Bret's luggage in the rear compartment of the roadster, listening to Commander Wright's last-minute instructions: "There's no reason why he shouldn't enjoy himself in moderation. Sports like swimming and golf are just what he needs to build up his self assurance. Maybe even the occasional night club, but he shouldn't do any drinking. . . ."

When they got away from San Diego's dreary suburbs and onto the coast highway, Paula drove fast. Their physical speed, their tangible advance through the whipping air, gave her the illusion of progress and the promise of fulfillment. But she was disappointed by Bret's attitude. After months in what amounted to custody he'd naturally feel awkward and shy on his first day in the outside world. Commander Wright had warned her to expect this. Still his continued silence worried her, nagging at the edges of her hope and threatening to spoil this sunny, blowing birthday of his freedom.

Snatching at any straw to make him speak, she pointed to a landmark she had often noticed before, the tall, leaning chimney of a brick kiln on the inland side of the highway. "I bet an immigrant from Pisa built that."

"I bet your pardon." His voice was heavy and dull. He hadn't noticed the leaning chimney. He hadn't even heard what she said, and she had to admit the warmed-over crack hardly deserved an audience.

His face, in the quick glance she stole at it, was as dull as his voice, a closed door standing between his thoughts and her. For all she knew his mind, unconscious of the sun and wind, was trapped and digging vainly in a lightless, airless mine of memory. She thought of the pit ponies that lost their eyesight because they never saw the sun, and for a hopeless instant she supposed that Bret was lost to her forever in those subterranean tunnels. She rejected her depressed mood as soon as she recognized it, and drove five miles an hour faster.

"I didn't hear what you said, Paula. Excuse me."

"It was a silly remark, and I couldn't possibly repeat it. Look, you can see the sea there between those two hills. Isn't it blue?"

He looked dutifully at the polished wedge of sea between the hills and looked away again. His eyes were bright blue and mindless, like the sea. His attention was turned inward, looking down the dark shaft. She didn't think explicitly that they were only a few miles from La Jolla, but his refusal to look at the sea shocked her. She was eager to show him all the things he had been missing, all the fine exhibits in the gallery of the world, and he wouldn't even look at their own memento—the Pacific.

"What's the matter, Bret?" her mouth said against her will.

"I've been doing quite a bit of thinking."

"But what about?"

"About what I should do."

"I thought that was all settled. You'll stay with me and see Dr. Klifter on alternate days. The rest of the time you can enjoy yourself for a change. I have to be at the studio in the mornings, and that'll give you a chance to do some work if you want to."

"I don't know whether I'll bother with seeing Klifter."

"But, darling! You have an appointment on Wednesday."

"I don't think my trouble is anything a psychoanalyst can help me with. It's too real for that."

"He isn't one of your old-fashioned dream doctors, Bret. He doesn't try to explain everything in terms of infantile bed-wetting. He knows the importance of the adult problems—"

"So do I. You see, I know what happened to my wife."

"You remember?"

His answer was slow in coming. It seemed to her that everything hung on it, like OEdipus' answer to the riddle of the Sphinx. The speedometer needle swung past seventy and hovered at seventy-five. The hair blew frantically about his head, but his face was as impassive as stone.

Would his face change at all if the car left the road and somersaulted down the bank of the arroyo? For a wild moment she played with the notion of giving the wheel a final twist and abandoning them both to the decision of mass and energy. A bright, windy day like this was as good a time to die as any. It would be fitting as the last gesture of her ending youth.

Almost before she was conscious of the moment, it was swept away by a deep rising hope. She caught a vision of herself years ahead living with her husband in a house with a garden and a big lawn where children and dogs could play. Her nerves leaned hard against the stability of that unbuilt house and that unconsummated marriage as she set her right foot on the brake. She turned off onto the shoulder of the highway and stopped the car. It seemed for an instant that the world had stopped, that the hills around them were waiting for a signal to move.

"Do you remember?"

"I don't remember her death, if that's what you mean. I remember marrying her in San Francisco."

"How do you know about her death? Did Dr. Klifter tell you?"

"He gave me these."

He showed her the bundle of clippings, and she felt like a dreamer whose recurrent nightmare has suddenly and incredibly become part of the real world. She looked into his face and trembled to know what was going on behind those steady eyes.

He felt most strongly a terrible pity for his dead wife, and a grinding shame. He had failed Lorraine, both living and dead. Living, he had abandoned her to violation and murder. Dead, he had forgotten her very existence, had sat snug and complacent for nine months in an animal world without memory, dreaming boy's dreams of happiness with another woman. But the irreparable past, more fatal than any predestined future because it was unchangeable and absolute, had caught up with him and embraced him from behind.

"That's what happened, is it?" His right forefinger tapped the papers he was holding in his left hand. She took them and looked at them, but she was so upset that she could decipher nothing but the headlines.

"Yes. Don't you—?"

"You needn't ask me again if I remember. I don't. I probably never will. The last thing I remember is flying in to San Francisco and landing at Alameda in the morning. They still haven't caught the man that killed her?"

"No. I've kept in touch with the police, and they're no further now than they were then. Bret?"

"Yes."

"Wouldn't it be better if you didn't let your mind dwell on this? I'm dreadfully sorry Klifter gave you those things. I shouldn't have let him have them. I should have destroyed them long ago."

"He did me a good turn. A better turn than you and Wright, keeping me in a fool's paradise."

"But this is in the past, Bret. It can't change the

present. It was sheer bad luck that it happened to us, and there's really nothing we can do about it."

"It happened to my wife," he said coldly. "To us only incidentically."

"I'm going to burn these filthy things." She had found her lighter in the snakeskin purse that lay between them on the seat. She lit it and applied the tear-shaped flame to the corner of the clippings.

He knocked the lighter out of her hand and took them away from her.

"Damn you!" she cried. "I don't like violence, Bret." She controlled her anger immediately and said in a neutral voice: "You might pick up my lighter and light me a cigarette."

"I'm sorry if I was rough."

"Forget it." She accepted the lighted cigarette he handed her as a further token of apology. "I don't understand why you wouldn't let me burn them though."

"There are some names I want—"

"You're not thinking of going to the police?" She tried to keep her voice steady and low, but terror lodged like a tin whistle in her throat and raised its pitch. "I went over the whole thing with them months ago, and nothing came of it."

"I don't suppose they'd be much help. I thought I'd look up this bartender Rollins. He might be able to tell me something."

"Rollins?"

"He was one of the witnesses at the inquest."

He riffled the clippings expertly, as if he had read them often enough to index them. "Here." He pointed to a paragraph at the bottom of a column:

> According to the testimony of James P. Rollins, bartender at the downtown eating-place and an acquaintance of the murdered girl, Lorraine Taylor was alone when she left the Golden Sunset Café. "She was alone and a trifle the worse for drink," Rollins put

it. "I offered to call her a taxi but she said to never mind. I figured she could make it all right under her own power."

"He said she left by herself." The whistle in Paula's throat made a discordant tune. "What more could he tell?"

"Probably nothing, but I want to talk to him. Don't you see, I don't even know who her friends were. I've got to try and understand what happened."

"But what are you going to do? There's nothing you can do."

"I have to prove that for myself. If I could find the man that was with her—"

"Are you jealous of a dead woman, Bert?"

"One might think you were jealous of her yourself."

She started the car and turned it back onto the highway. It was hard to see the road through the tears that had been brought to her eyes by the wind or by her sudden feeling of desolation. The present and the future were slipping away again, and in some way the fault was hers. She blamed her own stupidity and weakness.

The rode in silence through the green valleys and the barren hills, past the scrubbed whiteness of the sea resorts and the geometric forests of the Long Beach oilfields. The past slid along behind them on a trailer, as real as the buzzing, sprawling confusion of the Los Angeles suburbs. She longed for a city where she could submerge herself, ditch the trailing past, forget even the future. But the roaring blankness of Los Angeles was a comfortless backdrop to her loneliness.

It was loneliness that made her speak at last, though she didn't trust her voice.

"You didn't really mean it when you said you mightn't go to Dr. Klifter?"

"Didn't I?"

She lifted one hand from the wheel and touched his arm. "I don't think you should make any decisions when you're feeling depressed."

"I've got a reason for being depressed. I'm not going to get rid of it by fooling around with my childhood memories. I've got to act in the real world where the trouble started."

"Act?"

"My wife was murdered. God knows our marriage never amounted to much, but I owe her something. The least I owe her is some attempt to find the man that killed her."

The concrete pavement billowed before her eyes, and for the second time that afternoon she felt unable to drive. They were far out on the boulevard, so it was easy to find a parking space. She turned off the motor and leaned against his shoulder in a gesture of weariness and abandonment.

"You know you're not fit to plunge into a thing like that. They only let you leave the hospital on the understanding that you'd be in Dr. Klifter's care."

"I can't rest until I find the man that killed her. That makes no sense to you, does it? What makes no sense to me is your idea that I should waste my time telling my dreams to a psychoanalyst, instead of settling the trouble at its source."

"Are you sure this is its source? Even if it is, it can't be settled. You've got to learn to live with it."

He gave her a narrow look of doubt. "What makes you so sure?"

"The police spent months on the case. You can't do anything by yourself. I won't let you bury yourself in the past—"

"You sound afraid."

"I am afraid."

She pressed her face against the rigid muscles of his arm. Even in this moment of doubt and alienation she felt an undercurrent of pride in his strength, and gratitude that he had come back to her physically whole from the war.

"I won't argue with you any more," he said. "Give me the key to the trunk compartment."

"But you're coming home with me now? I told Mrs. Roberts to have dinner ready at seven."

"I'm sorry I have to spoil your plans. I've always spoiled your plans, haven't I? Give me the key."

"I won't!" She turned the ignition key and started the motor. "You're coming home with me whether you like it or not."

Before she had finished the sentence he was out of the car. She called his name and started after him, running awkwardly on her high heels. A seedy old man who was standing in the doorway of a cigar store turned to watch her, smiling knowingly. Bret was walking rapidly away, his wide blue shoulders perfectly impassive. She called once more, but he paid no attention.

She went back to the roadster and crawled in under the wheel. His white hat was a hundred yards away, moving steadily along the sidewalk. She watched it like a fading hope until it was out of sight.

CHAPTER NINE

As soon as she got home she went to the telephone in the hall and dialed a number. While the signal buzzed at the other end of the line she shut the door of the kitchen with her foot so that Mrs. Roberts wouldn't hear.

"Yeah?" A man's voice answered.

"Larry Miles?"

"Well, this is a pleasant surprise. I wasn't expecting to hear from you for a week or so."

"It isn't pleasant. Bret Taylor is in town."

"Do tell," said the softly modulated voice. "I thought he was all safely locked up with the other boys with the fantods."

"And it isn't funny. He may be looking for you."

"So what do I do? Take a powder?"

"Yes. Get out of town."

"It costs money to take a powder."

"You have the money."

"But nix, I had bad luck this week. No money. No money, no powder. Now a couple of C's would take me to Las Vegas. I got friends there."

"All right, you can have the money. If you'll get out of town for two weeks. I'll let you have it tonight."

85

"That's the good girl," said the engaging voice. "Usual time, usual place?"

"Yes. In the meantime, you know a place called the Golden Sunset Café?"

"But yes. Do I pay it a visitation?"

"Stay away from there," she said. "Do you hear me, Miles?"

"Excuse me while I adjust my hearing aid."

"I said this isn't funny. Bret Taylor's a big man, and there's nothing he wouldn't do."

"Be calm, my sweet, I heard you."

"Then bear it in mind."

She set down the receiver and climbed the stairs to her room. The solid floors and brick walls of her house seemed as insubstantial as a cardboard studio set. Even her bedroom lacked intimate meaning, as if its fourth wall were missing and the bed on which she flung herself stood in full view of the unfriendly city.

She got up and went to the mirror and looked at her face and didn't like it. She crossed the room to the great closet to look for a beautiful dress to wear. Her wardrobe appalled her. Gowns and sweaters, suits and scarves and skirts and coats, were garish and hideous, like masquerade costumes on hangover morning. Out of the thousands of dollars' worth of colored silk and cotton and wool, there wasn't a thing she'd be seen dead in.

When Larry went back to the bedroom the girl was sitting on the edge of the bed. In the excitement of the telephone call he'd forgotten all about her. Her red hair was tangled, but it shone prettily in the thin light that filtered through the closed blinds. When you looked at it in a better light you could see the darkness at the roots.

"You were gone a long time," she said. "Lover."

She stood up and came toward him with a dopey look on her face. Her navel and two nipples made a cartoon of another face, a long and mournful one. Whenever he saw that face instead of a body, he knew that he'd had enough of a girl. He let her kiss him, but he didn't kiss her back.

"What's the matter, Larry?"

"Not a thing."

"Who was that on the phone?" she whispered in his ear. Her arms felt sticky against the back of his neck.

"Business. I got irons in the fire."

"Such as?"

"*My* business, not yours. Listen, Fran, why don't you blow for now?"

"So you can keep a date with another girl."

"I said it was business."

"I heard the way you talked on the phone. You think I'm dumb?"

He looked straight into her eyes and grinned. "What do you think?"

"Who is she?"

"I thought I advised you to blow. Scram, fade, beat it, go away!"

She placed her right cheek against his chest and held on. "I'll go if you tell me who she is."

"All right," he said. "You want to do it the hard way." He took hold of her elbows with the air of a man removing an uncomfortable collar, broke her grip, and thrust her away.

"You shouldn't treat me like that," she said.

He took a step toward her. She backed away. "I'm going. But you'll be sorry if you treat me like that."

She put on her shoes and a tan polo coat. He followed her into the living-room. "Don't be like that, Fran. I told you it was business. I might have to go to Nevada for a couple of weeks."

"It's nothing to me," she said from the doorway, and added in a sweet and ugly voice: "Give her my love."

Listening to her footsteps go down the hall to her own apartment, he shrugged his shoulders. Fran had the idea that it was another woman, and there was no use arguing with a dame. It was another woman, all right, but Paula West was no she of his. West had a little too much class for him, not just the surface class that was his meat, but the kind that went way down out of sight like an iceberg and chilled you off at ten paces. She had quite a bit on the ball too, but it wasn't bright of her to tell him to keep his nose out of the Golden Sunset. He hadn't been near it for months, but now that he had a reason not to, that was exactly the bistro he was going to frequent.

He flung off his dressing gown and went into the bathroom to shave. He didn't have one of those three-way mirrors for looking at his profile, but by peering out of the corners of his eyes he caught a three-quarters view. He liked the way his chin jutted out from his neck in a clean line. Greek, but definitely. Not Greek like in the restaurant business, but like on monuments. They called him Adonis on the posters when he fought in the semifinals in Syracuse, and he'd looked the word up in the big dictionary in the branch library. His hair was light and wavy too, just like the picture of the monument in the dictionary.

Having applied brilliantine to his hair, suntan powder to his face, deodorant to his armpits, he started to dress in a hurry. He'd got out of the habit of wearing an undershirt before he got in the money, so the first thing he put on was a brown wool sport shirt. It had cost him fifteen fish, no less, but after all a fellow's wardrobe was kind of an investment. He felt he owed it to his looks to wear classy clothes. And some of his best pickups came when he was least expecting them. If you didn't want to run the risk of passing up elegant chances it paid to be on the make twenty-four hours a day.

He left the apartment building by the back door and took his car out of the garage in the alley. It was a Chevy coupé, the last prewar model, and the best thing about it was it was a souvenir from his hot-car days and hadn't cost him a cent. It was a pretty sweet little job after he tore down the motor, and it still ran like a dream. Everything ran like a dream for him these days, with a car and an apartment of his own, and good contacts in more ways than one, and a roll that would choke a horse. Well, a small horse. He wasn't so well heeled that another couple of centuries wouldn't come in handy. After he had the folding money in his poke he'd decide about Nevada. It might be better business to stay right here in L.A. and keep an eye on Taylor. There was no telling what might break, and if he played it smart and careful he could end up sitting very pretty.

The thought gave him such a lift that he was going fifty on Wilshire before he knew it. When he noticed the speedometer he slowed down abruptly to thirty. It wouldn't do to be caught speeding. Lawbreaking was the one thing he couldn't afford. He let fifteen or twenty cars pass him on the way downtown. Let the jerks stick their necks out, he was protecting his.

He found a parking place off Round Street, just around the corner from the Golden Sunset Café. Unless he missed his guess Taylor would be turning up there. It was the place that West was anxious for him to stay away from, and what other reason could she have? Before he went in he cased the joint through the star-shaped window in the door. The bar was loaded, and most of the booths were full. But no sign of Taylor. Maybe he missed his guess. In a way it was a relief.

He went in anyway and found an empty booth at the back. The smell of cooking grease from the kitchen reminded him that he was hungry. When the waitress discovered him he ordered a New York cut medium rare with French fried potatoes and a double order of onions, and a bottle of beer to drink while he was waiting—Eastern beer.

Halfway through the steak he looked up and saw Taylor walking down the aisle between the booths and the bar. The guy was in uniform, and in any case he couldn't forget that pan. He lowered his own face quickly. Not that there was a chance in a million that Taylor would know him. There was nothing to worry about at all. But he found that he couldn't eat the rest of his steak. The food he had already eaten had taken on weight and hung in his stomach like a piece of lead.

When he looked up again Taylor was sitting at the bar. All he could see of him was his broad blue back. Larry caught himself wishing that he and Taylor were alone in the room and Taylor's back was to him like that and he had a gun in his hand. He felt he was in pretty deep and it would take something like a gun to get him out. He brushed the thought away, but it kept coming back and spoiling the fun he got out of being himself.

CHAPTER TEN

Bret discovered that he didn't like people any more. He didn't like the middle-aged men with brown alcoholic faces going in or coming out of bars. He didn't like the sharp-breasted bobby-soxers chattering in gay circles, their eyes alert for autographs; or the older women like buxom birds in bright incongruous plumage. He didn't like the brisk, young, hatless men with their shirts open at the necks, and both eyes like one cyclopean eye on the main chance. Above all he didn't like himself.

Though his uniform was heavy enough and the waning sun was still warm, he stood on the corner of Hollywood and Vine and shivered with an immaterial chill. The high buildings and the roaring street and the quick inscrutable crowds appalled him. He had a shameful nostalgia for his hospital room, and then for Paula. The homesick pain turned into a headache that trampled on his skull like rubber wheels. The store windows blew in and out like flexible glass curtains, and the tortured air twisted and shrieked.

An empty Yellow Cab stopped opposite him, and he hailed it. It was something he could get inside. The first thing he had to do was find a room for the night. He didn't know for how many nights. Time and space had merged in an unreal continuum flowing past him in unnatural patterns. Tomorrow was Los Angeles, which nobody knew entirely and he knew hardly at all.

As he crossed the street to the waiting taxi, the traffic bore down on him from two directions like past and future impinging on the present. But the analogy was wrong. Time moved in a closed circle like a race track. He kept repeating himself in every lap. He was caught in a closed circle that only death could open. Game called on account of suicide.

"Where to?" the driver said.

"Do you know the Golden Sunset Café?"

"The place on Round Street? There's a Golden Sunset Café on Round Street."

"I guess that's it."

They drove across the city through white Chirico vistas, stark in the washed-out evening light, which led the eye only to other vistas like them. He felt relieved when they reached the older downtown section of slums and semi-slums. It was more human than the vast suburban wasteland, if only because a generation of men had lived there and died unwillingly. The headache still whined in his head like rubber tires, but they were receding. When the taxi let him out on Round Street he felt light-bodied and eager.

In each of the Venetian-blinded windows a sign in red neon script advertised cocktails. A painted sign over the door said: "Golden Sunset Chicken-Fried Steak and Jumbo Shrimp." He passed through the imitation-leather swinging doors into a roomful of people he liked better than the people at Hollywood and Vine. The evening had hardly begun, or perhaps the afternoon had not yet ended, but nearly all the stools along the bar were occupied. The people at the bar, most of them of indeterminate age and income, sat over their drinks in attitudes that were almost prayerful, though the café was noisier than any church. Blood brothers by virtue of the alcohol in their veins, he thought, they prayed to the god of the bottle for a brief, immediate heaven on earth; and the alcohol was transubstantiated into the stuff of dreams. He felt like an interloper whose presence had to be explained, but nobody paid any attention to him. A flashy young man in a back booth looked up from his plate as if he were going to hail him, but looked down quickly.

In the aisle between the bar and the plywood booths a very old man was performing a shaky two-step, in approximate time to a scratchy jukebox version of *Sentimental Journey*. Bret stepped out of his way and let him totter by, isolated and supported by the dream of youth that glazed his pale old eyes. He couldn't remember hearing the tune before, but its soft blue chords made counterpoint with the distant whining loneliness in his head.

He could understand the loneliness that had driven Lorraine to this place. Among the few things he knew about her he remembered that she loved crowds and jukebox music and the moist merriment of bars. The pain of remembering her was so intense that he wouldn't have been surprised to see her in one of the booths hunched over her drink as he had seen her more than once, with her chin resting on her hand and her dark hair swinging forward over her temples like loosely folded wings. There was a dark-haired girl in the second-last booth who might have been Lorraine until she turned to give him a once-over. He was disappointed and repelled by her harsh black eyes and carnivorous mouth; grateful too that the faces of the dead came back only in dreams.

At the rear end of the bar, beside the steamed window in the kitchen door, he found an empty stool. A large man, whose dirty white apron bulged out over his belly like a maternity garment, came to serve him.

"Scotch and soda?" Until he opened his mouth he hadn't realized how much he wanted a drink.

"We got no bar Scotch since the war." The bartender spoke with a heavy accent, underlining his words with his thick black eyebrows. "You want Black and White out of the bottle? Cost you sixty-five."

"Make it Black and White."

This man with the Central European accent couldn't be James P. Rollins. Rollins was an English name, or Irish. Maybe Rollins was the bartender at the other end of the bar, the dark thin fellow with sideburns that made his face seem narrower than it was.

When the big man brought him his change he left a dime on the counter and nodded toward the dark young man. "Is his name Rollins?"

"Naw, that's Rod. Jimmie ain't in tonight, it's his night off."

"You don't know where I can find him?"

"Not at home, I know that. Jimmie goes home to sleep. Just stick around, Mister. He comes in all the time on his night off. Gets a discount on his drinks, see? I don't do that myself. Never come near the place only when I got to, to work. I got a wife and family, that's the difference. Three kids I got, two *boys*, gonna be big like their old man." He thrust out his stomach in a gesture of exultant fatherhood.

"Good. What does Rollins look like?"

"Little guy. Curly hair. Bumpy nose, he broke it once. Just sit here, and I'll tell you when he comes in. By eight or nine he comes usually. You just wait."

"Rock and rye, Sollie," somebody shouted halfway down the bar.

Bret flipped the quarter in his hand onto the bar. Smiling and bowing, Sollie picked it up and bustled away.

Bret looked at his watch. It wasn't seven yet. He settled down to wait. When he had finished his Scotch he ordered another. By the time he finished his second the strong whisky had begun to soften and subdue his melancholy. The gilt-framed mirror behind the bar was like an archaic proscenium through which he watched the tragic life of the world. An aging woman with inexorably corrugated gray hair stood just inside the door in a tight flowered dress, searching the room with weary, myopic eyes. Somebody's mother, he thought in burlesque sentimentality, looking for her erring husband or her wandering son. The aging Hero watching for Leander drowned in his nightly Hellespont of gin. Or Penelope the floozie, loverless after all these years, seeking the lost Odysseus to show him the results of her Wassermann test. A little man in dungarees, who had been sitting beside Bret, slid off his stool and jerked his head at the woman. They sat down together in a booth below the frame of the mirror.

A man in the uniform of a chief petty officer had climbed onto the empty stool and ordered a rum-and-Coke. In the mirror Bret saw that the chief was watching him over the rim of his glass. He avoided the keen little eyes, having no desire to talk.

The chief spoke to him anyway, abruptly but not irrelevantly if you knew the Navy mind. "They tried to make an officer out of me, but I wasn't having any, and I can't say now I'm sorry. I had a chance to make warrant, but I went to the captain and told him I didn't want to be an officer, I didn't want the responsibility, and I wouldn't feel at home in the wardroom. He put up an argument, but I wasn't having any, and that was that. I went on eating in the chief's mess, best food on the ship."

"That's the way it was on our ship," Bret said.

He didn't want to talk to the broad-faced man, but there was no way out. One thing an officer shouldn't do was snub an enlisted man, and though the war was over and he'd been out of action for a long time, he was still aware of the obligations of his uniform and felt he owed some return for the privileges of rank. When the bartender brought the chief another rum-and-Coke, Bret insisted on paying for it and ordered himself another Scotch. It was his fourth, and he was beginning to feel it. It worried him a little, but the worry was soon submerged in the good feeling the drink induced. After all he hadn't had a drink in a long time, and he could expect to feel it. That was what it was for.

"You were on a ship, eh?" the chief said.

"For a couple of years. A jeep carrier."

"My name's Mustin." The chief thrust out a thick hand.

"Taylor's mine. Glad to know you."

Their handshake had some of the aspects of a hand-crushing competition, and Bret caught the inference. Mustin figured he was tougher than any officer, but he'd be glad to be shown.

"I was on an AKA myself," he said, "the last year of the war. Before that, a can. Right now I'm over at the Island, and if that shore duty holds out for two more years I got nothing to gripe about. Two more years I retire. I was ambitious once, but when I found my level I had sense enough to stick to it." He called the bartender and ordered two more.

Bret looked into his face and saw, as if under a magnifying lens, the harsh lines in the weather-beaten skin, the rum-washed eyes, the tired flesh relaxing on the neck beneath the powerful chin. They earned their retirement after twenty years, he thought. If they enlisted young enough they could retire at forty, but they were old men after twenty years in that iron world. Twenty years of beating around the bars and cat houses that fringed the shores of the two oceans. The old chiefs all looked the same: heavy, hard, shrewd, and somehow lost.

"Women are as crazy as hell," the chief said. After years of Navy bull sessions Bret found the abrupt transition as natural as speech itself. "Take the wife of a friend of mine for instance. He's a chief, too. Been all over the world, from Shanghai to France, and thought he knew his way around. Married this girl in Boston six years ago, and right now she's driving him nuts. When he got reassigned to the Pacific he brought her out here to live, and they got a little house in Dago, out in Pacific Beach beside the bay. This was before we got into the war, and for a long time he got home every night. Then when they sent the ship out, she was on the pineapple run, and he got to see his wife every two or three weeks. She was a good faithful wife, a religious girl too, but he told me she was passionate as hell. Not that he had any objections to that. He felt good about the deal.

"After Pearl Harbor, his ship got ordered to the South Pacific. She kept writing to him practically every day, but about a year after he left she sent him a letter that knocked him for a loop. It turned out she was all right when he was seeing her regular, but it was just too bad when she was on her own. She'd taken down her pants for somebody else, see, and she felt so awful about it, being a religious girl, that she just had to tell him. So she wrote and told him.

"This buddy of mine, his ship was operating in the Solomons then, and on top of his worry about his job this thing about his wife damn near drove him out of his head. Couldn't he forgive her? she says in her letter—she'd never do it again. She didn't want to do it that time, but she was drunk and she didn't know what she was doing till after, when she woke up in bed with this guy in his hotel room. He thought about it for a couple of weeks and talked it over with some of his buddies, and finally he got a grip on himself and wrote her a nice, decent letter. He said he felt like hell about the business, but he was never one to cry over spilt milk, and since she said she'd never do it again he guessed he'd have to swallow it and forget it as well as he could. A couple of months after that he got her answer. She said he was the best husband in the world, and all that crap, and she was going to spend the rest of her life trying to live up to him. Crap!"

"Maybe she meant it," Bret said. He felt sympathy for the woman. "One slip doesn't prove anything."

"Maybe one slip doesn't. But I didn't give you the pay-off yet. How's about another drink?"

"It's my turn." Though the story was interesting and he wanted to hear the end of it, a violent impatience was rising inside him. He resented being made the confessor at third hand of a sinner he had never seen, the depository of a monstrous moral problem of which he wanted no part. But he accepted the drink and the rest of the story that went with it.

"It was another year or so before my friend got home and then it was only for five days. His wife was wonderful to him, he thought. There wasn't anything she wouldn't do for him, and at the same time she was more religious than ever, going to Mass every bloody day, and stuff like that. He figured that the Church had straightened her out or something had, and that he'd done the right thing when he stuck by her. He went out again for another eighteen or twenty months and went through six or seven invasions, and she kept writing to him every day and telling him how much she loved him and what she wouldn't give to have him home with her in bed. In the spring of '45 he got his orders to shore duty and came home for keeps. His wife was waiting on the dock, and as soon as he took one look at her he knew that something was wrong. Wrong isn't the word. She hardly got him home before she told him that she'd done it again, she couldn't help herself. He was kind of under a strain, hadn't had any sleep since the ship left Pearl, and he gave her a swat across the face. She went to pieces then and came crawling to him on her knees, begging him to forgive her for her sins. 'Sins?' he said. 'How many times, for Christ's sake?' 'Fifteen or sixteen times,' she said. But she said she only loved him, and she swore to Jesus that if he'd keep her on, she'd be a good wife to him for the rest of her life now that he was home. The hell of it is he still loves her in a way, and he can't stand the idea of her opening up for a gang of lousy draft dodgers when he was at sea. When he looks at her he can't help seeing a bitch, and he's honestly afraid that he'll get so mad sometimes that he'll beat her to death. What's a man to do, Lieutenant?"

"I don't know," Bret said. "What would you do?"

Mustin's little eyes shifted and looked away. "We can have another drink."

Over his sixth Scotch—or was it his seventh?—Bret

considered the problem. He hated Mustin and his sordid story, yet he was as fascinated by it as if it had been a parable whose hidden meaning applied to his own life. Swayed heavily by the alcoholic pulse that was rising and falling in his brain, his imagination saw with hysteric clarity the pipes of sewage that branched like infected veins through all the streets of all the cities, the beast with two backs crying its rut in a thousand undomestic bedrooms, the insatiable appetite of female loins and the brutal meat that fed those blind, adulterous mouths. For the second time that day he felt the black wind blowing him toward extinction and the grave, that barren womb which feared no violation and threatened no second birth. A dead man, the foetus of the grave, futureless and untormented by even the first pricks of consciousness, merged carelessly with the filth and trash of generations, without a history or a thought to disturb the long serenity of blankness, the timeless gestation of the final dust. Because he wished himself dead he ordered and drank a double Scotch, and another, and another. They gave him back his desire to live, but turned his inward loathing outward.

He turned to Mustin, who had been silent for some time, and said: "This friend of yours with the unfaithful wife, has he been faithful to her?"

Mustin's face registered shock, as if Bret had named an unfamiliar obscenity. "Hell, no! He's been in the Navy all his life. He doesn't play around when he's at home, but when he pulls into Panama or Honolulu, naturally he takes it where he can get it."

"What's bothering him then?" Bret said roughly.

"You don't understand, Lieutenant." Mustin leaned toward him in his earnestness. "You don't get the situation. He married this girl in 1940 and thought he was getting a pure girl—you know, a virgin. Then when he's away fighting for his country she turns out to be nothing but a two-bit floozie. Worse than a two-bit floozie, without even the two-bits to show for it."

"You mean while he's away fighting for his country and incidentally picking up all the tail he can get on the side."

"What the hell!" exploded Mustin. "I'm a man, ain't I? A man's got a right to expect his wife to be pure, even if he isn't."

"Is this your wife we're talking about?"

Mustin lowered his eyes. "Yeah. I didn't mean to tell you."

"And you want my opinion on what you should do?"

"I don't know." Mustin's voice was thickened by alcohol and resentment. "You don't understand the situation. You never had a wife, did you?"

"That's none of your goddam business!" Bret cried. "I understand the situation well enough. You want to take it out on your wife for the rest of your life for doing what you've always done. Go home and tell her you're sorry."

The chief's broad mouth worked and spat. "To hell with you, Lieutenant! You don't know anything about it."

"I know more than I want to. You forced your story down my throat and asked for my advice."

"And what kind of advice did you give me? You can stick it!"

"Don't talk like that to me."

"Why the hell shouldn't I?" The chief's face was red and malevolent now, pushing closer and closer like an expanding balloon. "You're no officer of mine, and I say thank God for that! If that's the kind of ideas they teach you in a college I'm goddam glad I never set foot in one! Goddam college graduates pretending to be officers in a man's navy—"

In a movement that he neither intended nor controlled, Bret placed his open right hand against the angry face and pushed it backward.

"Hey there, cut that out now!" Sollie the bartender began to climb over the bar.

Mustin went down heavily on his back and got up

with his shoulders hunched and his fists extended. "Come on and fight like a man, you friggin' coward!" The sentence was punctuated by a blow on the side of the head which sent Bret reeling. He came back to attack the red face behind the fists, as if it represented all the unspoken hatred of enlisted men for officers, and all the venereal sin of all the ports.

A left jab to the cheek and a right cross to the side of the jaw put Mustin on his back for the second and last time. Bret stood over the fallen man, pleased to see the blood on his face. He heard a sound in the air behind and over his head, but it was too late to duck. A hard blow jolted the back of his head and split the room into many tiny fragments. It must have been a bottle, he thought as his knees buckled and he fell forward onto the floor. Then the black wind blew out the fluorescent lights.

CHAPTER ELEVEN

"Hold it," Larry Miles called, but he was too far away to interrupt the arc of the descending bottle. He had been watching the progress of the argument between Bret and Mustin, but its climax came so suddenly that it caught him flat-footed. He ran to the end of the bar, stepping over the two prostrate men, and faced Sollie the bartender, who was idly swinging the undamaged beer bottle in his right hand.

"Better give me that bottle, friend," Larry said.

"Who do you think you are? Who do you think you're talkin' to?"

"This officer is a friend of mine. I don't like to see my friends get hurt."

"Keep 'em from fightin' in this bar then."

"Should I call the cops, Sollie?" the other bartender said.

Half of the occupants of the café were watching the men on the floor from where they sat, but the other half had already lost interest in the fight. It hadn't been much of a fight anyway. Three punches and the usual pay-off with the bottle.

Mustin sat up holding his jaw, then climbed awkwardly to his feet. "You didn't need to sap the bugger," he said.

"You want me to call the police?" Sollie said.

"What the hell for? He didn't hurt me." Mustin dabbed at his face with a handkerchief and examined it suspiciously, as if a sly enemy of his might have stained it with red ink.

"What about this guy here?" Sollie said. "We can't just let him lie here on the floor."

"I'll take care of him," said Larry Miles. He kneeled down beside the unconscious man and looked at the bruise on the back of his head.

"Is he hurt bad?" Sollie asked with some anxiety.

"Naw, he'll be okay. He'd of come to already if he wasn't drunk. But we better get him out of here."

"You got a car—you know where he lives?"

"Yeah. I'll bring the car around to the front, and you can walk him out."

"You sure you're a friend of his?" Mustin said. "He's a set-up for somebody to roll him. What's his name?"

"Taylor," Larry answered smoothly. "Lieutenant Bret Taylor, USNR. I work for a very good friend of his."

"That's his name, all right," Mustin said to the bartender. He put his hand under Bret's shoulder, turned him onto his back, and raised him to a half-sitting position. "Well, let's get under way. I'm sorry this happened, but I guess it couldn't be helped. The guy's a little nuts, if you ask me."

Maybe you're righter than you know, Larry thought. Little did you know that you were talking to a fugitive from a padded cell, and little am I going to tell you. He brought his coupé to the front of the café, and looked up and down the street for his best friends and severest critics, the cops. Not that he knew them west of Syracuse, and not that they knew him, but he had a very special reason for wishing to avoid that pleasure. When he had made sure that the coast was clear he honked. Mustin and Sollie came out through the swinging doors with Bret dragging half upright between them. Larry opened the door and helped to haul him into the car. He could tell by the sound of his breathing, or thought he could, that Bret had come to from the knockout and passed directly into an alcoholic sleep.

As Larry drove away with the semirecumbent blue bundle beside him on the seat, the situation pleased him so much that he could have crowed like a rooster. Come to think of it, there was a good deal to be said for being a rooster, even if a rooster did have a hatchet waiting for him at the back door of the harem. Hell, he had a hatchet waiting for him too, but he was going to give the hatchetman a long and merry chase before they buried it in his own particular neck.

He drove toward Hollywood along the wide boulevard, lit by the starry neon symbols of glamour and nocturnal delight, past lighted store windows through which he caught glimpses of the smooth and glittering world he was one day going to crash. Just how the unconscious man beside him fitted into the picture, he didn't quite see, but it seemed like a good idea to take him along. He'd know what the guy was doing so long as he kept him with him, and the closer tab he kept on the new developments in the Taylor setup the better chance he'd have of keeping things running smooth.

More importantly, he felt, it pleased him to do the exact opposite of what Paula West expected. She'd ordered him to stay away from her lieutenant, and she was going to pay him to take the order. Only it happened he didn't take orders from anybody. He'd stick to Taylor like a brother as long as he felt any pressure the other way. Matter of fact, he was better than a brother, he was a good Samaritan. He spent the rest of the drive home alternately wondering exactly what a good Samaritan was, and trying to decide whether it would be safe to take a small cut, say fifty per cent, of the contents of Taylor's wallet. In the end he decided that it wouldn't. That Navy chief in the Golden Sunset was a pretty shrewd character, and he'd probably have a long memory. Larry thought he'd better play it straight with Taylor and waive the petty profits in the deal. He felt sure that that's what a good Samaritan would do, whatever the hell a good Samaritan was. Something like the Red Cross probably.

He drove straight into his garage and stopped the engine. Taylor was still sleeping, with his head wedged awkwardly in the corner of the seat. Larry took a flashlight out of the glove compartment and turned it on the closed face. There was a blue welt on the temple where the chief's fist had caught him, but otherwise he looked all right, snoring away as if he was home in bed. It gave him a pleasant sense of power to have Taylor in his car like this, completely helpless and unsuspecting in the dark garage. Even in sleep it wasn't the face of a man you'd want to fool around with. It was a strong, hard face, and Taylor was a strong, hard boy. The old one-two that put the chief to sleep was as neat as any he'd seen since the last time he fought himself. But right now the guy was as harmless as a baby. Larry slapped his face a few times in an experimental way, and damned if the guy didn't open his eyes and try to sit up!

"Take it easy, Lieutenant," Larry said.

"Who are you?" The words came thickly out of the dry and swollen mouth.

"Just a friend—a fine-feathered friend of the family. You feeling okay?"

"God, no! What happened?"

"You just got conked with a bottle, Lieutenant. The bartender put you out so's you wouldn't kill the other guy."

"I must've been tight. What in hell did I want to fight him for? Something about a woman—"

"Yeah, it usually is. You think you can walk up to my apartment? What you need is some shut-eye. It's no palatial abode, but you can use it if you want."

"You didn't tell me your name. I don't know you, do I?"

"The name's Milne, Harry Milne." It was a name he kept handy to use when his own wasn't convenient. "I was sitting in the café and I saw you get sapped, so

I thought I'd get you out of there before the cops came. These L.A. cops can be kind of unreasonable."

"You're very kind, but I can't impose on you—"

"Don't give it a thought. I like the way you punch. I did a little fighting myself at one time. Let's go, if you think you can make it."

Taylor was shaky, but he could walk without help. Larry took him in by the back door of the building and up in the freight elevator, because there was no point in advertising the fact that he had a guest. Women were another matter: the girls that visited him were good for his reputation. If they weren't, he visited them. But he didn't know yet what use he'd have for Taylor, so he kept his acquisition to himself.

Taylor was as meek as a kitten and didn't say a word until they were inside the apartment. Then he asked where the bathroom was and made a run for it. While Taylor was retching and cawing into the toilet bowl, Larry took his collection of autographed nudes off the wall and shut them up in a drawer. As long as things were sort of vague like this between them, he figured he might as well concentrate on making a good impression. The way things were going he and Taylor might end up as bosom pals. And that would be a belly laugh of the first water. He was a card, all right, a real wag out of the top drawer with bells on. In a way he regretted he didn't have an audience for this, but naturally there was nobody he could trust. He was so slick he barely trusted himself.

When Taylor came out of the bathroom, he looked ready for nothing but bed. Because there was no blood in his face his tan was a dirty jaundice yellow. His forehead was shining with sweat, and his eyes were still watering from the nausea. He was walking straighter though, and that was a good sign.

"Feeling better?"

"Yeah. I had some stuff to get rid of. I'm not used to drinking whisky."

"How's your head?"

"Not so bad. It doesn't seem to be bleeding."

"You're lucky the bottle didn't break."

"I suppose I am. Well, I'll be shoving off—"

"Don't do that, Lieutenant. Where do you want to go?"

"By the way, my name's Taylor." He shook Larry's hand. "I don't know how to thank you."

"Forget it. You're in no shape to go out again right away. You got a place to stay?"

"No, not exactly. But I couldn't possibly take up any more of your time."

"Hell, stay here. You can sleep in the other bed. Give me a reason why not."

"It's very good of you—"

"Nuts. I'd do the same for anybody, for any veteran, that is. The way I look at it we all owe something to you guys that fought the war." Jesus, what corn! But he certainly put some real sincerity into the lines.

"If you're certain it wouldn't put you out in any way. I admit I don't feel much like looking for a room tonight."

"Consider the question closed, Lieutenant. You can stay here as long as you like. You can even wear a suit of my pajamas—we're about the same size, eh? And don't say another word. Your bed's right in here."

By ten thirty Bret was sleeping again, and Larry slipped out quietly to keep his appointment with Paula West.

PART IV

DOOMSDAY

CHAPTER TWELVE

Bret's mind resisted the clarity of the morning. He half woke and half opened his eyes, painfully conscious of the shining razors of light that slid through the openings of the Venetian blinds. He closed his eyes again, groping for the severed ends of his dreams. But the shadows of the dream evaded him, fleeing backward down the tunnel of sleep like insubstantial ghosts. Consciousness took hold of him like an obstetrical forceps and pulled him into life by the head. The pressure of reality clamped on his skull was painful and somehow humiliating. He sat up in bed to shake it off, but the pain and humiliation hung on. The pain became distinctly localized in the back of his head, and the humiliation sank to the pit of his stomach and turned to nausea. He swallowed, with a throat as dry as sandpaper.

The memory of what he had to do came back in a rush, and he looked at his wristwatch. Nearly nine o'clock. He had wasted a whole night in drinking and brawling and sleeping, and was no nearer to the man who killed his wife than he had been before. He jumped out of bed and began to dress quickly.

He became aware that someone was watching him from the twin bed on the other side of the room. He half turned to see his roommate leaning on one elbow, smiling wryly in his direction. What was the man's name? Mill? No, Milne. Harry Milne. Their conversation of the night before came to him from a long way back, echoing against the hollow walls of his hangover.

111

"Good morning," the man in the bed said. "Have a good sleep?"

"Very. I've got to thank you for the use of your bed."

"Hell, that's all right. Use it as long as you want. I only sleep in one bed at a time."

"Will you let me pay you something?"

For some reason that seemed funny to Harry Milne. He laughed boyishly. "Christ, no! This isn't a rooming house I run. I do things for my friends that I wouldn't do for money." That was funny too, and he laughed again. "You're my friend because I like you. I make friends just like that"—he snapped his fingers—"and I drop 'em just as fast when the spirit moves me. Speaking of which, the spirit moved you pretty fast for a while last night. Hangover?"

"I'm as dry as a chip."

"Just a minute. I'll get you some milk in the icebox."

"Please don't bother."

"It's no bother." He bounced out of bed and padded across the room. Bret disliked that feline way of walking, but he repressed the feeling. The man was treating him like a brother, and he had no right to dislike him.

Larry saw that something was wrong. Did the guy know him after all? Had he made a slip? No, that was impossible. It was probably something very simple, like the guy not liking to be talking to somebody half in and half out of his underwear. The guy had nothing to be ashamed of though. He had shoulders like an ox. A little too heavy for a perfect figure (like his own) but he was fast too, a good, fast light heavy. Larry had a desire to fight the man, not that he had anything against him at the moment, but just because it would be interesting. Interesting for about thirty seconds, that is. With his ring experience he'd cut the guy to ribbons in six punches. And that would be kind of fun, too. Come to think of it, it would be a hell of a lot of fun.

Taylor picked up his blue trousers and started to put them on.

"Hey," Larry said from the doorway. "You can't wear those." He pointed at the triangular rip in the right leg. Even apart from that the whole uniform was streaked with dirt that wouldn't brush off.

"Damn it! These are the only clothes I have with me."

It didn't occur to him that he could go to Paula for his things. He didn't want to see her again until he had done what he had to do. For that matter, she'd probably phoned the hospital and told them he'd broken his parole, so to speak. Maybe they were already looking for him. The idea churned his stomach and made him angry.

"Look here," the other man was saying. "We're about the same size. You should be able to wear one of my suits. I'll take your uniform to the tailor around the corner. You can get it back today."

"No, I can wear the uniform."

"Don't be crazy. It's a mess. Here, try this." He tossed Bret a loose camel's-hair sports coat. "I got a wardrobe I hate to see going to waste. These slacks ought to fit you. They're a little too big for me. Go on, try 'em on."

Bret put them on out of sheer curiosity. He hadn't had civilian clothes on for years, and he'd never at any time worn a camel's-hair coat with a pair of light-tan gabardine slacks. "I feel like a sheep in wolf's clothing," he said.

"Say, that's pretty good." Larry laughed again. Bret didn't like his laugh any better than he liked his walk. There was something phony about all this pleasantness, and he didn't like to be put under an obligation by it. Still, it couldn't be helped unless he wanted to waste a lot more time.

Larry handed him a knitted brown tie and watched him tie it. "You look sharp." He went on talking as he dressed. "Pretty smooth coat, eh? It set me back eighty of them. Don't you go and get yourself into another barroom brawl, now. You wouldn't do that to me and my coat, now would you?"

"I can't wear your coat," Bret said sharply.

"Now don't be like that, fellow. I was only kidding. I want you to wear my coat, I'm crazy for you to wear it. Hell, I trust you, Lieutenant. You got to learn to recognize a friendly crack."

You talk too much, Bret thought, and I don't like your line of patter. What kind of cheap Hollywood character had he got tied up with? Still, this man had dragged him out of a bad situation and brought him home to sleep in his own bed. He couldn't very well snub him because he walked too lightly or because his conversation was fast and tinny. "You're the doctor," he said a little heavy. "I'm very much obliged to you."

Larry picked up the blue uniform and folded it over his arm. "I'll rush this over to the tailor's before you change your mind. If you want that milk I promised you, the ice-box is right through there." He pointed through the open door of the living room. "Hey, wait a minute. I almost forgot your stuff in the pockets." His fingers went through them rapidly, piling the things on the bed: handkerchief, comb, letters, address book, key case, wallet, some crumpled newspaper clippings.

"Give me that." Bret strode toward him and snatched the clippings from his hands, but not before Larry had seen what they were.

"Sure, sure," Larry said. The guy was beginning to get on his nerves, and he was even a little afraid of him for a minute. Taylor was supposed to be nuts after all, and you never could tell about a nut. Ordinary people, if you got in a jam with them, you could chop down and leave them lie, but there was something about a nut that drained the guts out of you. He was nuts himself to bring a nut like Taylor home to his apartment. What kind of a comic did he think he was, playing jokes on himself like that? The guy could have murdered him in his sleep.

"Sure," he repeated. "Don't get the idea I was trying to interfere with your stuff."

"I guess I was abrupt," Bret said. "It's just that I've

got some things marked in these papers. Food for thought," he added clumsily.

"Food for thought" is the word, Larry said to himself. His courage came flowing back and made him gay. Christ, the guy didn't know a thing, not a damn thing! He, Larry, knew it all and he, Larry, was sitting on top of the situation, playing a sucker with his own dice for any stakes he wanted to name. The dope Taylor had nothing on him and never would; it was the other way round and he was going to remember that. He nearly felt sorry for the dope, but not quite. It never paid to feel sorry for anybody.

He almost ran on his way to the tailor's shop, he felt so light and gay. He didn't know what irony was, but it was irony he was enjoying. Here he was, running errands for Taylor, of all people. Living with him, lending him clothes, sleeping in the same room. And all the time with a double century in his hip pocket for not laying eyes on the guy. If money really talked the way Paula West thought it did, he'd be in Nevada by now. But it was more interesting here and he had the money anyway, and plenty more where that came from. All he had to do was name it and he could have it.

He felt quite disappointed and betrayed when he got back to his apartment and found that Taylor had left. There was a note under a full milk bottle on the kitchen table:

Excuse me for running out, but I have some urgent business. Thank you again for everything, and please don't worry about your suit. B. Taylor.

Oh well, Taylor would be back, he could count on that. Taylor was the kind of guy that would have to come back to give him back his suit. He wasn't like that himself, praise God, but he'd met the type once or twice before in his life: the type that was so honest it hurt.

CHAPTER THIRTEEN

It was after ten when Bret reached the Golden Sunset Café. The place was deserted except for a few early barflies. It was chilly and desolate in the morning, like a fever patient who began each day with a low temperature and rose to a peak of delirium in the hot evening. The long room was like an image of his own hangover, run-down and almost empty, containing like a corrupt memory the odors of rancid grease and stale whisky spillings.

Fortunately neither of the bartenders who had witnessed the fight was on duty this morning. He had never seen the man behind the bar, a young man with thin round features like an emaciated infant's, wearing pockets of gray flesh, puckered like chicken-skin, under his indeterminate pale eyes. Rollins?

An excitement that gave him no strength took hold of the lower half of his body and shook him visibly. He sat down in the booth nearest to the door and reasoned with himself. He couldn't expect Rollins to be able to tell him anything. The police had questioned him long ago and found out merely that Lorraine had left by herself that night. Even if Rollins knew something more he had no reason to suppose that he could get it out of him. Still, the excitement would not stay down. It rose to his head and made him dizzy, so that Rollins's face, if it was Rollins, wavered behind the bar and the stagnant air in the room buzzed like an electric bell.

"What'll you have?" A waitress with a dark pitted

face had come out of the kitchen at the back and was standing calmly over him like an attendant.

He recalled that he hadn't eaten since noon of the previous day. "Fried eggs with toast?"

"Yeah. We got some bacon today if you want it."

"Good. And bring me a quart of milk right away." His dehydrated palate still regretted the bottle of milk he had left unopened, as a sign of his independence, on Harry Milne's kitchen table.

"A quart of milk?" The waitress raised one heavy black eyebrow. "You want it spiked with anything?"

"No, thanks. I'm a milk addict."

She stood and watched him drink it as if that were one for the book. Then she watched him eat his bacon and eggs.

"You were hungry," she said. They never tipped you in the morning, anyway—the jerks that came to this joint had to be boiled before you could peel a nickel off their palms—so you might as well act natural.

"Yeah," he answered. "I'm a food addict too."

She laughed even if he didn't, and what do you know, he gave her a buck and told her to keep the change. Things were looking up in the joint, and for a moment she forgot her varicose veins and almost stopped wishing that one of these A-bombs would explode directly over the roof of the Golden Sunset Café and destroy several square miles of L.A. with her in it.

"Is that James Rollins behind the bar?" Bret asked her.

"Uh-huh. That's Jimmie."

All but one of the barflies had drifted out. Rollins, who had just set up a boilermaker for the old man who remained, was manicuring himself with the blade of a pocketknife, scowling in bored concentration.

"Tell him I'd like to talk to him, will you? Over here."

"Sure thing," the waitress said, and went to the bar.

Rollins came through the little door at the front end and walked toward Bret with quick, jerky steps. "What can I do for you, my friend?"

"Please sit down."

"Why not?" He sat down facing Bret across the table, his pale round forehead still furrowed by the blank scowl.

Bret said slowly: "You were on duty here the night that Mrs. Lorraine Taylor was murdered."

A sneer of mental effort curled Rollins's lips and left them tight. "Yeah. Yeah, I was. So what?"

"I'd like you to tell me what you saw of her."

"You a cop?" he said in his quick monotone. "I already told my story to the cops."

Bret took a twenty-dollar bill from his wallet and folded it small. A rodent brightness glimmered faintly in the eyes across the table. "No, I'm not a cop. I'm interested in what happened to Mrs. Taylor."

"Jeez, bud, I don't know any more than you do what happened to her. She walked out of here that night, and that was the last I saw of her." Exerting a visible effort, he withdrew his attention from the twenty-dollar bill and looked into Bret's eyes. His gaze was as transparent and innocent looking as gin.

"Was she drunk?"

Rollins's wide mirthless grin showed a gold-capped wisdom tooth. "What do you think? You said you knew Lorrie. I never saw her sober, did you?"

"I didn't say I knew her."

"Oh, I caught you wrong. What's your interest then? Say, you're not writing one of these here true detective?"

"No." The interview was hopeless anyway, and there was no use in being cautious or discreet. "My name's Taylor. She was my wife."

"You her husband?" Rollins sat up straight, and conflicting emotions wrinkled his face like a sudden violent onset of old age. "I thought you was—" He regained control of his tongue.

"No doubt you did, but I'm not interested in what you thought." He unfolded the bill and smoothed it out on the table. "You're absolutely sure that she left here alone?"

"Sure I'm sure. I'm not the only witness either. You

know that. I wouldn't be holding out on a thing like that."

"You called her Lorrie—"

"Did I? That must've slipped out. You know how it is."

"I don't know. Tell me. Was she in the habit of coming here?"

"Yeah, sure. She was in here every couple of nights."

"Alone?"

"Of course alone," Rollins said very glibly. "The kid was strictly on the up and up. She was a little bit of a lush, but you can't hold that against her."

"I don't hold anything against her," Bret said, imposing a level tone on the violence of his feelings. "Was she a friend of yours?"

"Not what you'd call a friend," Rollins said uneasily. "Naturally I got to know her, with her coming in here all the time."

"Always alone?"

"I told you she was alone, didn't I? Look here, Mister, you got to excuse me, I got to get back to the bar. The boss'll be coming in any time." He cast a farewell glance at the twenty-dollar bill and rose to his feet.

"Sit down again," Bret said. "You've only got one customer, and he still has part of his drink." He took a second twenty from his wallet and laid it crosswise on the first.

Rollins resisted the magnetism of the bills, but it gradually drew him back to his seat. "I don't know what you want me to tell you," he said after an interval. "The kid was no floozie, if that's what you're trying to get at. I never had anything to do with her except for shoving her a drink across the bar. I never even knew her last name until I read it in the papers."

"You know very well what I'm trying to get at. My wife is dead. I'm trying to find out why."

"So why do you come to me? I'm not a prophet. I told the cops everything I know, and it wasn't enough to do them any good."

"Didn't she have any friends? You should be able to

give me some kind of a lead if she was in here nearly every night."

"Sure. She knew a lot of the regulars. Everybody liked her. One guy or another used to buy her a drink, but there was nothing to it."

In his eagerness to convince her husband of Lorraine's innocence, Rollins was overstating his case. Bret was encouraged to go on. "Who bought her a drink? Give me a name."

Rollins squirmed, but remained transfixed on the hope of a forty-dollar windfall. "I don't keep no diary, Mr. Taylor," he whined. "I got no list of names. I don't keep track of the customers' private life."

"One name. One man that knew her. One man that bought her a drink."

"I don't want to get anybody into trouble, Mr. Taylor. It's no crime to buy a girl a drink, and it's not my business what people do as long as they don't make trouble in this bar. For forty bucks it isn't worth it to me to make trouble for a customer."

"I have a lot of twenties in my wallet. How much?"

"Don't get me wrong, Mr. Taylor. It isn't the money I care about—"

"How much?"

"A hundred?" Rollins whispered.

"What can you give me for it?"

Rollins leaned across the table and spoke quietly, his eyes glancing sideways at the kitchen and the front door. "There's a guy that was interested in her. He tried to pick her up a couple of times, but she wasn't having any."

"When?"

"Oh, several times. He was in here the night she got killed. He wanted to take her home, but she gave him the old brush-off."

"Do you think that's worth a hundred dollars?"

"Wait a minute. I didn't tell it all yet. But for God's sake, Mr. Taylor, keep me out of this. I don't want to get anybody into trouble," he said, thinking of himself.

"Is that why you didn't tell the police?"

The drain of color from Rollins's face placed his pimples in relief. "You're not going to tell the police about this? I got no reason to think the guy had anything to do with murdering her. I wasn't going to throw him to the lions without a reason, was I?"

"A friend of yours?"

"No, not what you call a friend. If he was a friend I wouldn't be selling you his name for a hundred bucks, would I?"

Wouldn't you, Bret thought. He said: "You haven't told me his name."

"You haven't slipped me the hundred."

"Here's forty now." He pushed the bills across the table. "You said there was more to tell."

Rollins's hand moved like a quick white bird, and the bills were gone from the table. "You going to give me the rest?"

"When you tell me the rest of your story, and if there's anything to it."

"Yeah, but how do I know I can trust you?"

"You can trust me. The question that's bothering me is whether I can trust you."

"I'm telling you what I know. I can't do better than that."

"You're being slow about it. Go on."

"Well, this particular party tried to pick Lorrie—your wife—up like I said. She said she was going home alone, or something like that—I didn't hear her exact words."

"This was the night she was killed?"

"Yeah, a few minutes before she left. She went out by herself, just like I said, and this party got up and went out right after her. I didn't give it a thought then, but it came back to me when the cops were here the next day. I knew the guy had a car parked outside, and he might have gone out after her to give it another try on the street."

"Who is this man?"

"He's a fellow that comes in here sometimes. He used to be just another cheap grifter, but he made a lot of money during the war, and now he's opened his own cocktail lounge over in Glendale. He's still a crook through. The dirty bastard promised me a job over there, and then he turned around and gave the bar to Lefty Swift, a nance if I ever saw one."

"I see."

"What do you mean?"

"You're sure you're not simply trying to make trouble for him?"

"Honest to God, Mr. Taylor, trouble is the last thing I want. You asked me to tell you anything I knew, and that's what I'm doing. For God's sake, you won't tell Garth I told you?"

"Garth? Is that his name?"

"Yeah, Burton Garth. But you got to promise you won't tell him I told you. I don't know whether he had anything to do with the murder or not, but if he did I don't want any part of it."

"Unless it comes to court. Then you'll have to be a witness."

"Yeah, I guess so," he admitted reluctantly. "Do I get the other sixty?"

"If this Garth is a real lead. Otherwise not."

Rollins snarled in frustrated rodent fury: "That's not what you told me. You promised me a hundred."

"You'll get the rest after I see Garth. I told you you can trust me."

"Trust you?" Rollins laughed hollowly. "You promised me a hundred and slip me a measly forty."

"Calm down, or I'll take the forty away from you and hold it in trust for you." He stood up, casting a wide shadow across Rollins's side of the booth. "Where can I find Burton Garth?"

"How do I know I'll ever see you again?" Rollins muttered, half to himself.

"I said be quiet about that. Where is Garth?"

"He runs the Cockalorum over in Glendale. He's probably there now. You could give me your address, couldn't you?"

"I have no address," Bret said on his way out.

CHAPTER FOURTEEN

Normally he wouldn't have considered himself able to afford a taxi to Glendale, but money was one of a number of things he no longer cared about. He had between four and five hundred dollars in his pocket, with another couple of thousand in the bank, and he was convinced it was enough to see him through to whatever end he was blindly aiming for. Time was the only currency he was afraid to spend, for he felt that he had very little of that.

He spent the half-hour to Glendale leaning forward in his seat, as if to communicate some of his momentum to the cab. His need to be sure of something, combined with his unwillingness to face days or weeks of waiting and hunting down blind trails, had already half convinced him that Burton Garth was the man who had killed Lorraine.

The Cockalorum was half a block off East Broadway in the center of Glendale, a bar with a shiny new front of black-and-orange plastic. He told the taxi driver to wait.

Yes, Mr. Garth was in, said the soft-voiced young man behind the bar. He was in his office at the back. Just a minute and he'd call him.

"I'd like to talk to him in his office."

"Just as you say, sir. It's the last door on the right, the one beside the little girls' room."

The door of the office was partly open, and Bret knocked and stepped in. Garth was sitting behind a new steel desk that took up nearly half the floor space of the tiny cubicle. He was a bald-headed man in his forties, with a fleshy chin and neck that emphasized the sharpness of his nose and the smallness of his eyes. His sport coat was expensive and loud, matching the hysterical shrillness of his hand-painted sunset tie. Among drunks, morons, shills, prostitutes, and thieves, he might have passed for a man of distinction, so long as he had plenty of money in his pocket and spent it heavily. Bret hated him on sight, but that didn't mean anything. The man looked much too cautious and sly to commit a passionate crime.

"And what can I do for you, sir?" Garth said in a husky tenor.

"It's quite a story."

"Well, I'm pretty busy just now. If you'll just tell me what it is you want, Mr.—?"

"My name is Taylor. Lorraine Taylor was my wife."

"I don't know the lady. Should I?" His eyes shifted nervously, spoiling the effect of his smile.

Like all obvious bluffers Garth looked like a good subject for bluff. "I think you do," Bret said. "You were seen on the street with her the night that she was murdered."

"There must be some mistake." His voice was loud and firm, but he leaned across the desk and pushed the door shut. Bret felt a wave of mingled claustrophobia and loathing pass through his body. Had he come to the end already, shut up in a windowless cell with an aging tenor in a hand-painted tie?

"Won't you sit down, Mr. Taylor? I can't imagine what you're talking about, but I'd like to help you if I can. You say your wife was murdered?" He clicked his tongue irritatingly.

"On the night of May 23 last, at approximately ten

thirty. You were seen with her a short time before that. Do you deny it?"

"Of course I deny it." But he wasn't so angry and outraged as he should have been. "Look here, Mr. Taylor, just what are you trying to pull? Is this a joke?"

"It's not the sort of thing I make jokes about. And you don't seem particularly amused."

"Naturally I don't think it's funny when somebody comes in out of a blue sky and accuses me of being mixed up in a murder." His face groped for a smile but was frustrated again by his little, frightened eyes. "I don't even remember what I was doing on May 23."

"Yes you do. You were in the Golden Sunset Café that night. You asked my wife to let you take her home, and she refused. When she left, you followed her out and offered her a ride in your car."

"Somebody's been shooting you a line, Taylor, telling you wild stories about me. Who's been doing that?"

"You'll meet them in court," Bret said with sober emphasis. So far the man had made no slip, not verbally at least, but he was almost certain now that Garth was hiding something. "I want you to come to the police with me and have your fingerprints compared with the fingerprints that were left in my house."

"Go to hell!" Garth cried, in a voice that was as much a yelp as a bark.

"If you won't go to them, they can come here."

The anger that swelled Garth's face fizzled out like air from a leaking balloon. "Good God, man, you can't do that! I got a wife and kids. I just started up a legitimate business here. You can't bring the cops in on me like that for no reason."

"I had a wife too. Were you with her when she died?"

"No, I wasn't! Will you for God's sake sit down and listen to me, Mr. Taylor? You can't do this to me.

I never wished any harm to you or your wife either. Will you sit down and let me tell you why you can't bring the cops in on this? I made a lot of enemies when I dropped out of the racket, and there's nothing they'd like better than to see me railroaded to the pen."

"I'm not interested in your prospects. I'm interested in the truth."

"The truth is what I'm telling you, Mr. Taylor." His smooth brown pate was glistening like melting ice.

"You haven't told me anything yet."

"I'm an innocent man. You've got to see that. I wouldn't commit a crime like that, Mr. Taylor. I've got a daughter of my own almost as old as she was."

Bert leaned heavily across the desk and looked down into the upturned face. "You said you didn't know her."

"I knew her. Sure I knew her. I gave her a lift home that night. That doesn't make me a murderer, does it, if I gave a girl a lift home? You're a reasonable man, Mr. Taylor. I wouldn't be telling you this if I was guilty, would I? I'm as innocent as you are. Why don't you sit down?"

Bret sat down in the room's other chair, his knees squeezed uncomfortably against the end of the desk. Garth took a white silk handkerchief from his breast pocket and wiped his sweating face. "It's hot in here," he said hoarsely.

"I'm getting tired of waiting."

"Yeah, sure. I'm not trying to stall you, Mr. Taylor." He began to tell his story immediately, as if Bret had turned a dial. "I had no idea that the young lady was married, you've got to remember that. She was just a pretty girl I saw once or twice in the Golden Sunset Café, and I happened to get interested in her, in a perfectly innocent way. I was lonely—my wife and I aren't too happy together, Mr. Taylor—and she looked as if she was, and I thought it would be nice if we could kind of get together. Companionship is all I had in mind, I'll swear to that."

"You'll be swearing to all of this. Go on."

"It's quite true what you said, I was in the Golden Sunset on the night of May 23, and I happened to see her there. Frankly speaking, she was a little the worse for drink, and I became a little alarmed for her. The Golden Sunset is not a first-class restaurant, and some of its customers are unscrupulous, to say the least. Well, to make a long story short, I offered to take her home in my car. Being a married woman—only she didn't tell me that—she quite naturally refused, and naturally I bowed myself out. It would've been better for me if I'd forgotten the whole thing right then and there, but I couldn't, Mr. Taylor. I was worried about her and kept my eye on her. I told you I have a daughter of my own, going on eighteen. Mrs. Taylor couldn't have been much older—"

"Skip the paternal element," Bret said harshly. "You don't expect me to believe that."

The melting face congealed in hypocritical shock. "You don't accuse me—?"

"I said skip it. It turns my stomach."

Garth wiped his face again. Bret could see the wet discoloration spreading through the soft silk collar that encircled the fleshy neck. Perhaps the room was hot, but he himself felt cool and bloodless. His heart pounded in his chest like a dry stick on a drum head. "Go on," he said.

"Well, after a while I saw her go out. She was kind of unsteady on her legs, and I didn't know if she'd be able to get home by herself. I followed her out and offered her a lift, and she accepted it. She didn't complain about it, but I got the idea that she was feeling a bit sick. She was looking a bit under the weather. Anyway, I drove her straight home. The ride seemed to do her good, because when we reached the house she was looking much better. As a matter of fact, she graciously invited me to come in for a drink, and I, like a fool, accepted. When we were climbing the steps of the front porch a man came running out of the front door. Mrs. Taylor was a little ahead of me, and he pushed her out of the way and came at me. He was a big guy and terrifically strong. I tried to fight him off, but he sailed into me like a lunatic. He caught me off balance and knocked me backwards down the steps. When I tried to get up he jumped me again and knocked me down on the sidewalk. I'm no coward, Mr. Taylor, but I knew I was no match for him, so I ran out to my car and drove away."

"Why didn't you call the police?"

"I thought of doing that, but you see they're not such very good friends of mine. And you've got to remember my position, Mr. Taylor. I was perfectly innocent, but you'd never get anybody to believe that. You don't believe it yourself, and there's my proof. I'm a married man, and in a way I had no right to be there. I thought this man was her husband. He came out of her house like I said, and besides, when he pushed her she said something that made me think it was her husband."

"What did she say?"

"I forget exactly. Something like 'Take your hands off me, you bastard!' Anyway, she talked as if she knew him. I thought sure it was her husband or I wouldn't have run out like that. And naturally I would've called the police. But I didn't catch on that it wasn't her husband until I read about it in the paper next day and found out that her husband was an officer in the Navy. This guy was in civilian clothes."

"What did he look like?"

"He was big, like you, I told you that, and I think he was pretty well dressed. I think he was kind of good looking, but I didn't get much of a look at his face. It was pretty dark, and everything happened too damn fast. One minute I was flat on my back on the sidewalk, and the next minute I was in my car and lamming out of there."

"It still seems funny you didn't go to the police," Bret said slowly.

"I explained that. I thought it was her husband."

"But next day when you found out it wasn't? When you read in the papers that she had been murdered?"

"I couldn't go to the cops," Garth whined. "Say I told them about this guy and they couldn't find him. Where would I be then? I'll tell you: halfway to the San Quentin gas chamber for a murder I didn't commit but couldn't prove I didn't."

"That's where you are now, isn't it? Are you sure this man that beat you up ever existed?"

"For Christ's sake!" Garth said wildly. "Look at this if you don't believe me." He pointed to a long white seam just below and parallel to his right eyebrow. "I almost lost my right eye where the guy socked me. Half of my eyelid was flapping loose, and I had a lump on the back of my head as big as a goose egg."

"I have scars too. They don't prove anything."

"All right! All right! I'll prove it to you. Come over to L.A. with me. Right now?"

"What for?"

"I can prove that I'm telling you the truth. My face was bleeding so bad after that guy hit me I went straight to the nearest doctor, and he put eight stitches in my eye. Maybe you know him. Dr. Ralston? He lives only two or three blocks from your house."

"I don't. I never lived there. But we'll go and see him. I've got a taxi waiting outside."

Garth stood up and took a pearl-gray fedora from the top of the safe in the corner behind him. Sitting behind his desk, he had given the impression of size, but when he stood up Bret could see that he was short and stout, a nervous little man whose legs were stiff with fright.

Garth was jumpy and ill at ease in the taxi. He tried to start a conversation about his family, which Bret said nothing to encourage. When Garth finally subsided they rode in silence. Bret kept his face turned away from the other man and wearied his eyes with the monotony of the streets they were passing through. The houses were stucco or frame, one-storied almost without exception, sitting on narrow fifty- or sixty-foot lots that allowed room for a square of lawn in front and a clothesline and tiny garden at the back. The cramped houses, hardly more individual than a row of rabbit hutches, stretched under the noon sun in a cityscape of quiet resignation. Led on by the westering dream, he thought, the latter-day pioneers came from all over the country, all over the world, to homestead in the flat and empty finality of these streets.

"Caesar Street," Garth said suddenly. "Say, that's your street. That's your house there, isn't it?"

"Is it?" He twisted his head around and caught a glimpse through the rear window of the stucco bunga-low Garth was pointing at. It looked like any other house he had never seen.

Garth looked curiously into his face. "Don't you know your own home?"

"I told you I never lived in it. My wife bought it when I was at sea." It occurred to him suddenly that he had seen the house before, the night Garth had been there. That night was still a blank to him. Every-thing he knew about it he knew at second hand, but that wasn't Garth's affair.

"Anybody living there now?"

"I don't know." But of course there wouldn't be. "No, it's empty."

"I thought I saw a dame in the back yard, but I guess it was the next house."

Soon afterward the driver let them out in front of a two-story frame house identified by a weatherbeaten wooden sign attached to the railing of the porch: "Ho-mer L. Ralston, M.D."

"It's a good thing I saw that sign," Garth said. "I was bleeding like a pig, and the doc said a blow like that can kill a man sometimes."

A cardboard sign on the front door invited them to "Ring and Walk In." The dingy waiting-room was lined with patients sitting stiffly under the cold eye of the nurse who presided at a table beside the door. She looked up as they entered.

"Yes?"

"We want to see the doctor," Garth said.

"The doctor is very busy. You'll have to wait your turn."

"We didn't come here for treatment," Bret put in. "It's a legal matter."

She shrugged her starched shoulders in fussy resignation. "Sit down, please. I'll see what I can do when he finishes with his patient."

After a strained five minutes they were ushered into the consultation room. The doctor, a big, dull-faced man in his middle fifties, was sitting sideways at the desk.

"What can I do for you gentlemen?" he said without rising.

"You remember me, doctor?" Garth asked eagerly. "When you put some stitches in my eye last May?"

The doctor regarded him for a moment. "Let's see, you came in here after office hours, didn't you?"

"Yeah, that right. It was about—"

Bret interrupted him: "Let the doctor remember for himself."

The doctor looked from one to the other through thick spectacles that made his brown eyes seem froglike and suspicious. "You haven't been having trouble with your eye, Mr—?"

"Garth. Burton Garth. No trouble at all, doc. My own doctor, that's Clark over in Glendale, came to look at it a couple of times, and he took out the stitches—"

The doctor cut him short. "If there's nothing more, Mr. Garf, I have patients waiting."

"There is something more," Bret said. "A crime was committed at a certain time last May 23. Garth claims he was in your office at that time."

The doctor took off his glasses and revealed his little, tired, old eyes. "You from the police?"

"I'm investigating the matter privately. If you can check the time Garth was here?"

"Don't you remember when I came here, doc? You couldn't forget that. I had blood all over my shirt."

"I remember you all right. I was just going to bed. Let me see, it must have been around ten o'clock at night."

"Would you swear to it?" Bret said.

"I believe I would. Yes, I would. It was about ten o'clock."

"And the date?"

The doctor turned up the palms of his thick hands in a helpless gesture. "I hardly ever know what day of the week it is. But you can check my records." He raised his voice and called: "Miss Davis."

A young nurse came in by the rear door. "Yes, doctor?"

"Remember the night I called you back to help with this gentleman's eye? Mr. Garth, is it?"

"Do you remember what time the doctor called you?" Bret asked her.

She turned up her eyes to the ceiling and stood still for a long moment. "Yeah," she said at length. "It was a little after ten, maybe ten after. I paid special attention to the time because it was so late."

"Check the date in the files, Miss Davis. These gentlemen will be in the waiting-room." The doctor waved away their thanks and pressed a buzzer under the desk.

A few minutes later Miss Davis brought them a filing card that fixed May 23 as the date of Mr. Garth's visit.

"Well, that's that," Garth said as they left the house. With the pressure of fear removed, his personality was already beginning to expand obnoxiously. "Maybe next time you won't be in so much of a hurry to accuse innocent parties."

"You're lucky," Bret said grimly. He was angered and humiliated by the fact that this corpulent little rat had picked up his wife on the street, even though it appeared that Garth had done no more than that. Garth was the kind of civilian that all servicemen hated, the man who stayed behind and made his pile out of the war; too old or sick to fight, but not too old or sick to pursue women and cuckold their absent husbands. But in this case Garth himself had been a victim. Bret's mind shifted to the vague man who had knocked Garth down the steps.

"Can you tell me anything more about this man? Did she call him a name or anything like that?"

Garth turned and faced him beside the waiting taxi. "I don't think so," he said slowly. "I told you as much as I know. He was big and good looking and he had on pretty snappy clothes. Sport clothes, I guess you'd call them. I think he had light-colored hair, but it's hard to tell at night. Look here, Mr. Taylor, I got to get back to my business."

"Go ahead. I know where to find you if I want you."

Over his shoulder Garth gave him a last worried look. Then his tweedy, fat body was swallowed up by the taxi and trundled away. Bret stood on the curb for a moment to get his bearings, and then turned back on foot in the direction of Caesar Street.

CHAPTER FIFTEEN

A middle-aged woman was sitting on the porch of the white bungalow, looking very much as if she belonged there. He looked at the number again to make sure that it was his. 1233 Caesar Street; he'd addressed too many letters there to be mistaken. But the house evoked no image or sense of place. Even his knowledge that Lorraine had been murdered here and that he had found her body, while it hung upon his mind like a clock weight and had motivated all his actions during the past day and night, seemed wholly external to him, as unassimilable as the strange woman on the porch of his empty house.

He turned up the walk, and she rose to meet him, a heavy woman with a tired face framed by short, graying hair. An ill-fitting blue flowered cotton dress was wrinkled over her body, which time and gravity had conspired to ruin.

"Hello," she said. "If you're selling, there's nothing I want to buy, unless it's nylons, that is." She looked down at her thick, naked legs. "Haven't had no stockings for six months, that's how my legs got so chapped, I always did have a delicate skin."

"I'm not selling anything. My name's Taylor—"

"You don't say!" Her slack face tightened in pleased surprise. "Don't tell me you're Lieutenant Taylor?"

"Yes."

"Well, I declare! I thought you was—" She dropped the end of the sentence like a hot potato and raised her voice to a shout. "Pa, come and see who's here. We got a visitor, you'd never guess." She winked at Bret and whispered hoarsely: "Don't tell him who you are. Let him guess. He'll be surprised." She added to herself, or to the world in general: "Lord knows he needed something to sober him up!"

"I'm a little surprised myself," Bret said stiffly. "I thought my house was empty."

"You mean to say Miss West didn't tell you? I knew she didn't want to bother you when you was sick, but now you're all better again, it's funny she didn't tell you. She was here a little while ago too. Anyway, if you ask me for my opinion, and I don't care if you knew about it or not, it was real nice of you to let us stay here like this."

"Not at all." It was grotesque and incredible, but he was beginning to suspect that this woman was Lorraine's mother. Lorraine had told him in San Francisco that her family was in Michigan, but she had evaded detailed questions about them. He'd guessed that she was ashamed of them, and he hadn't inquired too closely into the story of her father's being one of Henry Ford's right-hand men and he could get her a very good secretarial job any day, only she'd rather make her own way in life and have her freedom.

The woman let her tongue run on with the unself-consciousness of the poor, the people who have nothing to lose. "I hope you're not thinking about moving in here yourself right away? Pa hasn't found a job yet, and the way he's been hitting the bottle since Lorraine passed away, the good Lord knows when he's ever going to—Pa!" she cried again. "You gone to sleep in there?"

A man's voice grumbled and whined inside the house, and two feet stamped heavily on the floor.

"He *was* asleep," she said. "I never saw a man that could sleep as much as Joe Berker. He was on the graveyard shift the last year at Willow Run, and it got him in the habit of sleeping in the daytime. Now he sleeps at night besides. I told him more than once he ought to get himself examined for sleeping sickness, but I was only kidding. It's probably just that wine he drinks all the time. He calls it *vino* since we came out here. You'd think he was a dago or something—"

Her voice ran down like an unwound phonograph when she perceived that Bret was no longer listening. The name "Berker" had confirmed his guess that this woman was his mother-in-law, and the knowledge filled him with an ugly sorrow. So this was the family he had married into; this gross and aging hag was the substitute he had acquired for the beautiful dead mother of his childhood. Then he became aware of the woman's worried eyes watching his stony face. The awareness was like a dash of cold water. Snap out of it, you fool! He told himself. Byronic melancholy was the opium of the intellectuals and the last refuge of little minds. Snap out of it and act like a man!

"Mrs. Berker." He held out his hand to her, fumbling awkwardly for words that would compensate for the contempt he had been feeling and had scarcely tried to hide. "I'm glad to meet you. Lorraine often talked about you—and wrote about you." Lorraine had mentioned her once or twice: the prominent clubwoman and gracious hostess, a little stuffy and straitlaced as befitted her social position, though she had been a successful career woman before her love marriage to the rising young executive Berker—

Her hand, thick and coarse-grained, gripped his warmly. "Mercy me, don't call me 'Mrs. Berker,' call me 'Ma'! I guess we're still related even if poor Lorraine ain't with us any more."

"Yes," he said. "Ma." The bitter bleating word incredibly brought tears to his eyes.

He was glad that she had turned away from him to peer through the dirty window into the house. "Look at that now. He's gone back to sleep in there. Excuse me a minute. I'd ask you in only the parlor's in such a mess."

She pulled open the screen door and paused in the doorway for an instant before she went in. "Just sit down and make yourself comfortable."

"Thank you."

For an instant of no more than a heartbeat's duration the angles of her cheekbones and jaw had caught the light in such a way that he saw her resemblance to Lorraine. The line of the skull was there beneath the aging flesh, tender, pathetic, and clear, like a sculptured fragment of youth caught out of time. Just for that instant, it seemed that Lorraine had come back and was standing before him, heavy from the grave and cruelly aged by the eternal hours of death.

It was no more than a trick of the eye perhaps, but it had the stern and general sadness of deep insight. He saw more clearly than he ever had before that flesh was as grass, youth and beauty impermanent and precious, life itself a perishable good to be used while it lasted, generously and honorably. Even in pain and sorrow there was a sweet excitement, a sense of life; and a hard-earned pleasure like a boxer's in submission to the punishment of time. The one irreparable loss was that of life itself. Lorraine was the one to be sorry for, the dead girl married to oblivion, and not the worn-out woman who had borne and survived Lorraine, who carried still within her declining body the talismanic fragments of youth.

The slamming of the screen door set a period to his thought. He sat down in the worn canvas chair his mother-in-law had vacated, and watched the street, trying to throw his attention away from himself, away from Lorraine and her family and the past, from all the bottomless spiral anguish of the world. Women were walking babies and shopping-carts on the pavement. A delivery boy went by on a red scooter that emitted a continuous stuttering raspberry. A paralytic old man passed the house inch by inch, walking quadrupedally with two canes. He was so old and thin, with the withered skin hanging in folds from his obstinate skeleton, that it was a wonder he could move at all. He stopped at regular intervals to rest and to look up at the sun, the emergency battery on which he depended for another month or another year of life.

Bret smiled at the old man with the sun in his face, half from sympathy and half from envy. At that age the only problem was to live, to wring another drop of energy from food and weather, cover another city block by minuscule degrees, reconquer the lengthening space between waking and sleeping. For a while in the hospital he had been like an old man himself, an old man or an infant, who needed nothing but sleep and food, until his resurgent mind had driven him like a cruel angel out of the Eden of the physical life. It was a hard rebirth into the adult world. He still had a nostalgia for the warm and quiet places of mental death, and a wildly yawing inclination to self-pity. Only in the last week had he been able to face the memory of Lorraine, to recognize the difficult fact that he had destroyed himself through her. No doubt the years of the war had softened him up for the final blow; Lorraine was the one who had found the fatal crack in his defenses.

For a while after their quick and ill-timed marriage he had held the truth at bay. During the first weeks of separation, when the one physical love of his life had been cut off and left him raw and sensitive to the masculine life of the ship, it had been important to him to keep her image intact. She was a good girl, a devoted wife, perhaps a little harebrained, but basically as sound and sweet as an apple; this was the icon that gave him strength in return for his uncritical worship. Then time and distance, working together like acids in combination, dissolved the fabric of the illusion. The memories of their marriage day and their drunk honeymoon fell into the patterns of reality, and her infrequent letters came to fill in the blanks. She was selfish. She was a liar. She was lazy and discontent. She was a fool. And he, who had married her between drinks on time he owed to another woman, was worse than a fool.

Even so he had enough integrity and objectivity to try to make the best of it. If he had made an unfortunate marriage so had she. He answered her letters dutifully. He sent her as large an allotment as he could afford, and, when she asked for it, the money for the down payment on the house, more than half the money he had saved for writing his book when the war ended. He tried to keep his thoughts loyal to her and to give her the benefit of whatever doubts he had. Meanwhile he lived on his nerve and by his sense of duty. Neither of these was enough to sustain a man indefinitely in the operational area. The last seven weeks before the ship was lost there was an average of eight or ten general quarters a day, but they didn't disturb him much because he had given up sleeping almost entirely.

Now there were no more doubts. Lorraine's morals, like her mind, had been as light as a net balloon. The only mystery was why he had not seen it on the first night. As casually as any tart she had let him pick her up and take her to his hotel room. He suspected he was only one in a long series of lovers that did not end with him, a second-class private in the nocturnal army that had bivouacked on her young *mons*. Perhaps the man who had caught her on this porch with Garth had been her steady lover, but even if that was so, she had been willing to be unfaithful to him, and with such a creature as Garth. He couldn't hate the girl who had betrayed him and then died suddenly in the midst of her light sins. She had nothing to lose but her life, and she had lost it. Her body was already half turned to dust. All his hatred settled on the man who had been the last to violate her bed, the shadowy man who had taken her life as hostage to his jealousy.

The screen door creaked behind him, and he jumped up to meet Lorraine's father, who was framed in the doorway like a living portrait of depression.

"That's your son-in-law, Pa. Lieutenant Bret Taylor, no less. Go on out and make yourself sociable."

Berker pushed the screen door partly open and slid through. He was wearing a faded denim shirt that gaped open at the neck, showing the mat of wiry hair on his chest, a shade darker than his gray stubble beard. His breath was winy, and the whites of his swollen eyes were wine red. He held out a grime-cracked hand with the forefinger cut off below the first joint.

"I'm glad to meet you," Bret said as they shook hands.

"Same here. I guess you noticed I got a missing finger. Lost it in a corn cutter in 1915. I went down in the silo to look for it, but couldn't find it. Probably made pretty good ensilage at that—"

"Now, Pa, the Lieutenant don't want to hear about that." She smiled apologetically at Bret. "It's the first thing he wants to tell them about whenever he meets anybody."

"Wouldn't want them to think I was born that way," Berker said moodily. "I stuck it in a little hole in the corn cutter, and *whish!* I'd of been more careful if I'd knew how hard it was to get a job with a finger missing. I don't suppose you got any job worries though. That fiancée of yours looks pretty well heeled if I ever saw one—"

"Be quiet, Joe," his wife said sharply. "Where's your manners?"

"You want a slug of *vino?*" Berker asked, by way of remembering his manners. "I got a half-gallon jug, and it's only half killed."

"No, thanks. Did you say Paula was here?"

"Yeah, a couple of hours ago," Mrs. Berker said. "She was looking for you. She was even talking about putting an ad in the papers, but I told her it wasn't anything to get so worked up about. Joe here used to drop out of sight for a month at a time when he was your age, and then he'd turn up like a bad penny as dapper as you please."

"Do you have a phone?" He resented Paula's persistent interference, but if she was worried about him he'd have to get in touch with her.

Berker grinned sheepishly. "We got a phone, only it's disconnected. We don't know nobody in this burg anyhow, so it don't make no difference. Why in hell we ever drove across the country to come and live in a burg where I don't know nobody and can't even get a job—"

"You be quiet," his wife snapped. "If you got no job, you know whose fault it is, and you wouldn't want your eldest daughter lying dead with nobody to tend her grave. Besides, Ellie's making some real nice friends in the store, which is more than you can say for the trash she knew in that trailer camp. Ellie's our other daughter," she explained parenthetically to Bret. "You'd like her. If we was still in Michigan, you know as well as I do, Joe Berker, Ellie wouldn't of stayed with us any more than Lorraine."

"Good riddance, then."

"That's a fine way to talk. You want the lieutenant to think we ain't good parents to our children? Where would we be now if it wasn't for Ellie? Answer me that."

"Go to hell!" He went in and slammed the door behind him. His diminishing voice complained as he retreated: "I made better money in my life than any snip of a girl—"

"Don't pay no attention to him," the woman said. "He hasn't been the same since Lorraine—and then they closed down the plant. He's worried about Ellie, thinks she's getting fast ideas from the girls at the five-and-ten. He was worried about Lorraine the same way after she ran away to Hollywood. I told him a girl as pretty and bright as Lorraine was sure to land on her feet and maybe even make a success in pictures, but he always said she'd be ruined. It certainly turned the tables on him when she sent us the letter as cool as you please that she was married to a full lieutenant in the Navy. I hope you'll get a chance to meet Ellie some day soon. I don't think she's quite as pretty as Lorraine, but a lot of people do. She's a blonde, taking after Joe's mother, and her hair is naturally wavy. She never had a permanent in her life."

Bret's sympathy had receded in spite of his efforts, and left his original stony contempt. "I have to be going," he said brusquely. Wasn't one of your daughters enough for me? Keep your Ellie with the naturally wavy hair, and keep the house and the furniture and the memories in it.

"Goodness gracious," she said, "why don't you sit down and relax for a bit? Don't let Joe put you off like that; he don't mean anything. We haven't even had a real visit yet, and I know you want to see Lorraine's pictures. She was the cutest kid you ever saw when she was little. Did she ever tell you she had red hair when she was a toddler? I got a lock of it in the trunk."

On the point of departure he was struck by the full realization that these were the steps where Garth had been attacked, that was the door from which the murderer had come. Perhaps Lorraine had known the man for years, perhaps her mother knew him. Mrs. Berker was standing at the door holding it open, waiting uncertainly for some encouragement from him to fetch her mementos of Lorraine. Gradually her arm relaxed and let the door swing shut.

"I'm looking for a man Lorraine knew. He may have had something to do with her murder."

"Now who would that be?" The whimpering question ended in a high-pitched sob, and a devil-mark grimace slid over her face and curled its sagging lines. "It was a terrible thing—a terrible thing to happen to my little girl." The word "murder" had swept away her defenses, leaving nothing, no childhood snapshots or locks of hair, between her and the fact. She stood blinking like someone staring into a blinding light.

"I don't know his name. I haven't even a good description of him."

"Somebody in Michigan? She had a lot of friends in

Michigan, but most of the fellows she knew at Dearborn High were real nice boys. They wouldn't do a thing like that."

"Did she know a big man with light hair? He probably had some money, he wore good clothes. About my size, I think, and he liked fighting. It's possible his hair wasn't blond."

"It couldn't be Sammy Luger? He was a big blond boy she went out with, and he had good clothes. Only I heard when we left Michigan he was still in the army. He was a sergeant in Berlin."

"Then it couldn't be Sammy Luger, could it?" He instantly regretted the savage irony of his tone and softened it. "Do you know of anyone else who fits the description?"

"She knew lots of big men, but she never ran around with the brawling kind. She was with a nice high-class crowd at Dearborn High. When she was in her junior year they elected her the most popular girl in the class. I guess it went to her head, sort of. She was doing real good in her studies but she quit before she finished up the year. She should have stayed with her ma and pa," she lamented, "and then this wouldn't of happened. It wasn't anybody she knew that did it. It was one of these Los Angeles sex maniacs, a Mexican or a nigger. They'll do anything to get a white girl. Many's the time I've thought it'd been better for her if she'd grew up as ugly as a witch."

Her sobs became more frequent, the rhythmic peaks of sound in a ululation that included fragments of sentences in its pattern: ". . . a good girl . . . nobody she knew . . . kill the dirty animals . . . killed my girl."

Bret opened the door with his left hand and with his right arm around her heaving shoulders, propelled her into the house. The front door opened directly into the living-room. Berker was on his back, emitting strangulated snores, on the beaten chesterfield at the far end of the room. Beside him on the newspaper-covered floor a green glass jug stood open. The patches of floor that were visible between the dirty newspapers had lost their hardwood finish and were acquiring a patina of grease and grime. There were several teacups full of cigarette butts on the cracked glass tray of the coffee table, but most of the ashes and butts of recent months were piled in the disused fireplace, from which they had gradually spread like volcanic ash across the room. There was a tangle of peach-colored woman's underwear on the radio, and in the opposite corner a lint-covered mop was leaning. The armchair beside the door, ripped as if by a butcher knife, was spilling its cotton guts into its lap.

Mrs. Berker sat down heavily. Her sobbing continued, unconsciously synchronized with her husband's snores.

"I'm sorry," Bret said to her bowed head, "for everything."

He ran through the door and away from the house.

CHAPTER SIXTEEN

He caught a cab at the boulevard.

"Where to, bud?" the driver asked as he leaned back to open the door.

Paula's address was on the tip of his tongue, but he didn't give it. If he went to Paula they'd have the old argument over again. For all he knew there were a couple of male nurses waiting at her house to wrap him in wet sheets and ship him back to the hospital. No telling what lengths an anxious woman would go to. Certainly he'd have to phone her as soon as he got the chance.

The light had changed, and the driver threw in the clutch. "Which way?" he said impatiently.

Almost without thinking, Bret gave him the address of Harry Milne's apartment. His choice of destination was easy to rationalize. All day he'd felt like an impostor in Milne's clothes, a naval officer masquerading as a small-time Hollywood character. He was convinced that he'd be able to think better when he got into his blues again. The meeting with his unexpected tenants had jolted him and set his mind revolving in interminable circles. Paula seemed to have a finger in all of his affairs.

When his taxi drew up in front of the long stucco building, he noticed a roadster, the same color as Paula's, parked in front of it under a palm. No doubt she'd be here to anticipate him if she'd known he was coming, but even a woman's intuition wasn't as clairvoyant as that. When he had climbed the stairs to the second floor and found the door of Milne's apartment, his doubt of her clairvoyance was shaken. A woman's voice that sounded very much like Paula's was speaking in angry tones on the other side of the door. He knocked at once, and the angry voice was hushed.

Henry Milne, large and confident in his shirt sleeves opened the door carefully and stood blocking the aperture with his body. "Hello, I wasn't expecting you." He stepped out into the hall and closed the door behind him.

"I came to give you back your clothes."

"They're at the tailor's," Milne said quickly. "It's got a sign, 'Mac the Tailor,' up that way, just around the corner to the right. You leave my suit with Mac, and I'll pick it up later, eh? I'm busy right now, you know how it is." He tried to wink gaily and conspiratorially, but there was no humor in his shallow, strained eyes.

In the face of this anxiety to get rid of him, Bret delayed his departure. "I'm grateful to you for helping me out," he said blandly. "If I could—"

"Look, friend. I got a dame in here. You want to do something for me, you can blow. Leave my clothes at Mac's. I trust you."

His attitude was awkward and tense, with his right hand behind him on the doorknob. The door jerked open suddenly and almost threw him off balance. He shrugged his shoulders and stepped aside to make way for Paula.

"Bret! Where on earth have you been?"

She was as well groomed as usual, but her skin was pale and translucent and her eyes had a faintly mongoloid puffiness, as if she had spent a bad night. She wore a tall garish hat and a yellow wool suit in militant contrast to her mood.

"I've been around. Mr. Milne was good enough to lend me some clothes—"

"Mr. Milne?" She glanced at the man beside her, who was leaning with false nonchalance against the wall. It seemed to Bret that the look they exchanged was electric with hatred or some other emotion. "Oh," was all she said, but her breath came out with the syllable and lent it a hissing quality.

"Look here, Lieutenant. You just shed the vestments at Mac the tailor's like I said, and we'll call it even." He made a move toward the open door.

"Just a minute. I left my purse in there." Paula stepped into the apartment ahead of him and came out a moment later with a yellow handbag. The door was shut behind her, and the bolt of the lock snapped home.

"What's the matter with him? Did you accuse him of kidnapping me, or what?"

"How in hell did you get mixed up with that man?"

"It was perfectly natural," he said unpleasantly. "I lost possession of my faculties last night, just as you might have expected, and he brought me home with him. But what brought you here?"

"I was looking for you. I was awake all last night—"

"You might have saved yourself the trouble. I admit my mental history has its blank spots, but I'm not exactly a character out of Krafft-Ebing."

"It isn't that, Bret. You told me you were going to look for the murderer. There are some terrible places in this city, some terrible people." Involuntarily her eyes turned to the closed door. She took his hand and drew him along the hall.

He answered her as they descended the stairs: "Biologically, at least, I'm better equipped to deal with them than you are."

"I don't know whether you are, darling. I'm a woman, and my brain is ever so tortuous."

"You haven't explained how you got here."

"Haven't I?"

She said nothing more until he had paid off his taxi and was sitting beside her in her car.

"I know you don't like me to do things like that, but you've no idea how miserable I was. I finally thought of going to that wretched café, and one of the bartenders knew that Miles—this man that took you home. Why didn't you come to my house? I spent most of last week furnishing a room for you."

"I'm sorry—sorry you were worried. I intended to phone you when Mrs. Berker told me you were looking for me."

"You were there, then?"

"I wanted to see the house. I thought it was empty."

"You don't mind my letting them stay there? It was going to waste."

"They can stay there forever as far as I'm concerned." He leaned forward and looked soberly into her face. "You're a pretty good woman, aren't you? A generous sort of woman."

"Am I?" She laughed lightly and uncertainly. "I suppose I feel I owe something to the people I've hated, even to their relatives."

"Did you hate Lorraine?" He was painfully conscious that this was the first time her name had been spoken between them. The mere name seemed to add a dimension, a bitter edge of reality to their complicated situation.

"Yes, I hated her," she answered bluntly. "Not since her death, but before, when she took you away from me." She started the engine with a furious roar. "Damn you, you get me talking like somebody out of nineteenth-century drama! Can't we stop thinking about Lorraine?"

"I can't."

The roadster was still at the curb, and she shifted to neutral and let it idle. She turned toward him in the seat and spoke to him in a small, coaxing voice he had never heard her use:

"You'll come home with me now, won't you? You

have your appointment tomorrow. It's funny to think it was only yesterday you left the hospital. It seems ages, doesn't it?"

"You'll have to cancel the appointment. I have other things to do. I've found out more in twenty-four hours than the police did in all those months."

Her hand went to her mouth and hovered there as if to guard what she said. He had an impulse, which he failed to obey, to touch her face, smooth the fear out of it.

"What have you found out?" she said finally.

"I've found out that there was a man with her, definitely."

"The police know that."

"They haven't got a description of him and a witness who can identify him. I have." He gave her Garth's description of his assailant. "The police don't know anything about a man like that, do they?"

"No," she said through her nervous fingers. "All they have are the fingerprints." Abruptly she started the car and drew away from the curb.

"Wait. I have to change my clothes. He said the shop was around the corner to the right."

She swung so wide at the corner that she nearly struck a car going in the opposite direction. He had to remind her again to stop at the tailor's.

As he took off Harry Milne's clothes behind the faded green curtain at the back of the steamy shop, he wondered why Paula had called him Miles, and why she was acting so strangely. He folded the gabardine slacks over a wire hanger and draped the camel's hair coat over them. When he had put on his pressed and mended uniform, his eyes lingered for a moment on the glad rags he had discarded. In the dim light of the ceiling bulb there was something eerie about the empty coat, like a deflated and truncated man hanging against the wall. His imagination stirred to life and added a face to the man. Milne (or Miles?) had light hair and was handsome enough in a way. Milne had a bit of a tin ear, and that meant a background of fighting. Milne was a big man about his own size. Beyond that, Milne had shown an unexplained interest in him. Was it because Milne knew he was Lorraine's husband?

He rushed past the bowed little man at the pressing machine and out of the shop so fast that Mac had to follow him into the street to collect his money.

"Sorry, I'm in a hurry," he said, and overpaid the man a dollar. Mac was unimpressed. He shuffled back into his shop, muttering resentfully to himself.

"A hurry about what?" Paula said when Bret climbed into the car. "And where's your hat? Remember the time on the beach the commander reprimanded you for taking off your hat?"

There was more tension in her voice than the harmless reminiscence warranted, and he felt that she was trying to throw him off the track. The memory of their first weeks together, La Jolla and the bright nostalgia of love pulled at his mind, but he shook them off.

"My hat's still back in Milne's apartment. Drive around the block, will you, Paula?"

"I thought we were going home."

"Not yet."

"Don't go back there, Bret. I don't like that man. I don't trust him."

"I don't trust him with my hat."

"But you've got another in your luggage, haven't you? Or you can buy one."

"I want that particular hat. Among other things."

"Other things?" Her hands were tight on the wheel, though she still hadn't started the engine.

He knew that she guessed his intention. Through some obscure feminine channel she had reached the conclusion that he suspected Milne, or Miles (it wasn't surprising that a murderer should use an alias). He knew too that she dreaded another meeting between them. But it would only start another argument if he brought the conflict into the open.

"My black tie," he said. "He's still got that too."

She refused to accept his superficial version of the situation. "You mustn't go back there, Bret. I forbid you to go back."

A vein of anger swelled in his head. " 'Forbid' is a strange word to use. It hasn't become part of your official vocabulary yet."

She looked at him blankly as if her mind was elsewhere, occupied with an internal pain or a remote disaster. The first time he had spoken to her at Bill Levy's party she had seemed like an old friend. Now he saw her as a stranger. Her brown hair was too neatly arranged under her vivid hat. There were tiny dry lines in her forehead and at the corners of her swollen eyelids. Her orange lipstick was unnaturally bright against her pale skin, and so heavily applied that it seemed to weigh down her mouth.

"Still, I forbid you," she said.

"That's unfortunate." His own face felt stiff and dry. There was a knot of pain behind his eyes, a focus of anger and desolation. He put his hand on the door handle and pressed it down.

"Wait," she said sharply. "You've done enough to spoil my life. I'm not going to let you do more if I can help it."

He stayed where he was, shocked and outraged by her frankness, which struck him like a blow below the belt.

"You may not feel that you owe me anything—"

"I know I do," he said, but she didn't pause in her furious speech.

"I feel that you do. You've given me damn little to go on, and I've been as faithful to you as a wife could be. Do you understand that I've lived by you from the first day? I've worked for our future together, and I've suffered for it. I have the right ask you to stay in this car and come home with me."

"But why?"

"I can't tell you why."

"Then I have the right to refuse. I know what I owe you, but it doesn't mean that you can give me orders. I have other debts to pay, and I've got to pay them in my own way." He knew that what he was saying was melodramatic and unfair, but he was beyond caring. His brain was ice cold and boiling at the same time, like a cup of liquid air.

"Is your dead wife more important than our future?"

Her voice was weary and defeated, as if her subterranean thought had gone to the conclusion beyond the spate of words. Still, she had to finish the dialogue. Every scene had to have its dialogue, even if weeping, screaming, beating her fists on the windshield and on the hard man's face beside her would have been a truer expression of her feelings.

He too had said it all before, and said it again: "My future won't begin until I've licked the past."

"You can't lick the past. It's done. It's finished."

"I'm licking it now."

She essayed an ironic laugh that came out as a screechy titter. "You're knocking yourself out, you mean, and for no good reason. For God's sake, and mine and your own, let me drive you home with me."

"I can't. If you don't see that, there must be very little about me that you do see."

"I love you, Bret. Does that mean anything to you?"

"Love can be mistaken."

"Are you ready to call it off then?"

"Not unless you force me to. I do know that we can't set up housekeeping in an open grave."

"Words! You can twist words any way you like, but I thought the thing we had was stronger than rhetoric. I thought you loved me. If you don't I'm not interested in trying to force anything. Do you love me?"

A moment before, her face had been the face of a stranger, an unknown, harried woman in whose car he happened incongruously to be sitting, arguing for the right to master his difficult life. He looked into her face again and saw that it was his lover's, familiar and dear in every line. He had loved her from the beginning and would never love anyone else. He was ashamed that she had had to ask him.

"I do love you," he said. "But can't you see there are things more important than love?"

"What things are more important than love?"

"Justice."

"Justice! You think you can go and find justice like a lucky horseshoe? A four-leaf clover in a field? Look around you and tell me where you see justice, except in books and movies. Do you see the good people getting the breaks and the bad people getting the dirty end of the stick? The hell you do! There's no Hays Office to censor life and make all come right in the end. Everybody has to make his own life turn out, and you know it. That's all I'm arguing for, Bret, for you to keep your head out of trouble. You try to make things over, and you'll only beat out your brains." But before he answered she knew that her angry words were as ineffectual as she had said words were.

"You must think I'm pretty futile." The irony he had intended was lost in his sense that he had spoken the truth. In self-distrust and confusion, still shaken by her statement that he might spoil her life, he clung to his stubborn will and the brittle mood that sustained it.

"I think you're strong," she said, "but you don't know what you're up against."

"Your friend Milne? Or is the name 'Miles'?"

"He's not my friend. I detest him."

"And you're afraid of him, aren't you? You haven't told me why."

"I'm afraid of a man who is capable of anything."

"I'm not," he said flatly.

It was no use talking any more. She could never be made to see that he had to do what he was doing. He had no right to love or security until he had settled the question that dragged on his mind. Only action could remove the deathly magnetism that drew him back and down and distorted all his certainties—even his certainty of Paula.

Through the dingy window of his shop Mac the tailor

watched Bret as he got out of the car and walked away. The woman's head turned slowly after him and stayed like that until he was out of sight. But she didn't try to follow him or say a word. From the expression on her face it looked to Mac as if she was in bad trouble, with no idea of how to get out of it. He was just as glad when she drove away, because it made him feel kind of low to see a pretty woman stood up like that and looking so blue.

CHAPTER SEVENTEEN

There was a pay telephone in the drugstore on the corner, tucked away behind the prescription counter. Bret couldn't find the Cockalorum in the directory, but Information gave him the number.

Garth himself answered the phone: "Yes?"

"This is Bret Taylor. I want you to come over to L.A. right away."

"For what?" The high voice was suspicious and resentful.

"I want you to look at a man."

"I'm busy, Mr. Taylor. I got things to do besides chasing all over the county—"

"Don't you want to catch the man that beat you?"

"Sure I do, but I don't want to get in more trouble. I can't afford it."

"You can't afford to have me give your name to the police."

"You wouldn't do that, Mr. Taylor? I co-operated with you, I helped you every way I could."

"You can come here and help me some more." He described the location of the store. "I'll wait here for you, but I won't wait forever."

"I don't like this."

155

"You don't have to like it. I'll be waiting." He hung up.

There was a lunch counter in the front part of the store, and it reminded him that he was hungry. He slid onto an empty stool and ordered a sandwich and a glass of milk. Then he bought a paper and returned to his seat to read it. The small black letters formed words, and the words were strung together in sentences, but the sentences had no meaning. There were more legible sentences written in acid between the lines.

In the first flush of recognition he had had no doubt that Milne was the man. But as his feelings cooled and shifted his point of view, the circumstances that pointed to Milne were revealing secondary patterns. Whether his hunch was right or wrong the obvious thing to do was to call in the police and give them the facts he had uncovered. But he rejected the idea. They'd only be a further complication, and he didn't trust the police, who had failed Lorraine so miserably. He had failed her himself but he was resolved not to fail again. He trusted himself, and no one else, to remain incorruptible and see the thing through to the end.

His mind was crouched and tense like a sprinter waiting for the gun. His look returned again and again to the doorway, yet when Garth appeared he didn't recognize him immediately. The little man had changed to an off-white double-breasted suit with a black shirt and a yolk-yellow tie. He stood just inside the door, a sawed-off travesty of sartorial splendor, while his mobile little eyes glanced back and forth and finally settled on Bret. Bret threw down his unread newspaper and went to meet him.

"You think we're going to head into trouble?" Garth said as they went out. "This guy's a killer, remember, if you got the right one, which I doubt—"

"Save it until you see him."

"Where is he?"

"Half a block from here in his apartment."

"You expect me to walk right in on him? What if he knows me?"

"You'll be all right."

"Maybe. I don't take chances on that boy." Garth patted the side pocket of his coat significantly.

"That won't be necessary. We'll do it like this." The plan, which he explained as they walked toward the apartment, was intended to give Garth a look at Milne without being noticed himself. Bret would knock on Milne's door while Garth waited down the hall. When Milne opened the door Bret would keep him there until Garth could walk past the door and downstairs to the lobby.

"Yeh, but if he knows me? He might jump me."

"I'll hold him."

"If this is the guy he won't be so easy."

"I can hold him. Come on, this is the place."

"I don't like this."

But he followed Bret through the lobby and up the carpeted stairs. The upstairs hallways were deserted, dimly lit by windows at their remote ends. All the doors were closed. Somewhere behind one of them a record of the "Pastoral" Symphony was being played. Its sweet rustic gaiety echoed forlornly through the building, bounding disconsolately against the doors and partitions and dying in the walled air.

"Go down to the far end and start back after I knock. We don't want him to hear us coming together."

Garth walked away with fear prodding him in the kidneys, a dapper and pathetic silhouette against the light from the window at the end of the hall.

Bret followed Garth halfway down the hall and knocked on the door. From the tail of his eye he saw Garth moving toward him, and simultaneously he heard light footsteps inside the apartment. His throat felt tight, as if constricted by the pressure of converging events. The bolt of the lock was shifted, and Milne opened the door.

"You again?"

"I'm sorry I have to trouble you. You have my hat and tie."

"Oh. Yeah." He looked narrowly into Bret's face. "Is there anything else, or is that the works?"

"Let me see." Garth was to his left and behind him, out of his range of vision, but he could hear Garth's footsteps falling softly on the carpeted floor. Milne's eyes had shifted from Bret's face and were looking beyond him into the hall. Garth's footsteps were directly behind him now, following each other very slowly, so that it seemed his heart beat many times between the footfalls.

"Won't you let me pay you for all your trouble?"

The pale eyes returned to him. "Hell, no. I'm glad to help you out. What happened to the girl friend?"

"I don't know."

"Maybe she's waiting for you, eh? How's about coming in and have a drink? It won't do her no harm to wait while you have one little drink."

"No, thanks." He allowed his impatience to enter his voice. "May I have my hat and tie? I'm in a hurry."

"Why, sure, certainly. I was just trying to be a pal." He left the door open and returned a moment later with the white-covered hat and the black tie. "You want to look in a mirror to put your tie on?"

"No, thanks. Not now."

"You leave my suit at the tailor's like I said?"

"Yes. Thanks for everything."

Bret walked away quickly without looking back. Not until he reached the head of the stairs did he hear the door softly close.

Garth was waiting in the street, jumpy with nerves. "Is that the man?"

"Now look here, Mr. Taylor. I saw him at night and it was quite a while ago. I think it's him—"

"Will you swear to it?"

"Let's get away from here. He might come out." He started away on his short legs, moving so fast that Bret had to run to catch him.

"You know it's him then, don't you?"

"I said I *think* it's him, but I can't swear to it. There's no use dragging me into court, because I won't swear to anything."

"Forget about the law, can't you? That man slugged you and killed my wife. Didn't he?"

"It's him all right," Garth said reluctantly. "Only remember what I said if you drag me into court. I co-operated with you to the best of my ability—"

"Give it a rest. And lend me your gun."

"What you want a gun for? You better call the cops and let them handle it. Give me a chance to pull out of here, and call the cops."

"I didn't ask you for advice. I asked for your gun."

"You can't have it. It's a damn good gun, and I need it in my office."

"You can buy another."

"It's not registered. It cost me fifty bucks. Give me one reason why I should hand you fifty bucks."

"Here." They had reached the corner in front of the drugstore. Bret stopped him and held out a fifty-dollar bill.

"It's not registered, I told you. It's not so easy to re-place."

"All the better for both of us."

Garth took the money and looked at it. Then he swung past Bret in a half circle as calculated and neat as a veronica. Bret felt the sudden weight of metal in the pocket of his blouse, and almost as tangibly he felt a new respect for Garth. The little man had unsuspect-ed talents.

"Thanks."

"Don't thank me, boy. You try to use that rod and you'll burn your fingers for sure."

"I don't expect to use it. I want it for moral sup-port."

"Moral support for what? I still say call the cops. Give me five minutes to get out—"

"Maybe you're right. I will."

"Uh?"

Garth left him without a backward look or a good-bye and scurried across the road to his parked car. Bret stood on the corner, smiling grimly, until Garth's yellow convertible had nosed out into the stream of traffic and merged with it. Then he went back to the apartment building he and Garth had just left. For reasons there was no time to examine, he had no intention of calling the police.

For the third time in an hour he knocked on the door. This time there was no answer. An entire minute ticked off in individual seconds while he listened and waited. He knocked again more loudly and was answered by another thirty seconds of silence. He knocked so hard that the thin panels reverberated under his knuckles like a drum. Once more he waited very briefly, and then his patience ended. Stepping back across the hallway, he ran against the door and burst it open with his shoulder.

The living-room contained nothing but the afternoon sunlight sluiced through the tilted slats of the Venetian blinds. He closed the door behind him and looked around the room. A row of nude photographs on the wall to his right: "To my old friend Larry . . ." "For Larry, who has what it takes . . ." A heavy armchair crouched in the corner beside a cabinet radio-phonograph and a table covered with piles of scrambled records. He looked behind the chair, behind the chesterfield, and went through the rest of the apartment: the kitchen, remarkably neat and clean; the windowless little bathroom, where he had been sick the night before; the bedroom with its two unmade beds, and nothing under them but rolls of fluffy dust; the closet full of clothes hanging in quiet ranks, with no man behind them. He had made one visit too many, and Milne had taken the hint.

Standing in the empty bedroom with Milne's possessions all around him, in his nostrils the piny odor of some sort of masculine scent, he was overwhelmed by his nearness to the man who had killed Lorraine. He had spoken to him, been touched by him, slept in his

room with him all night, even worn his clothes. He
had been in intimate contact with a murderer and had
seen in him nothing out of the ordinary. Nothing
worse than cheapness and vulgarity, qualities that had
seemed harmless enough in a person who was helping
him out. The cheapness had been moral bankruptcy,
and the vulgarity had been viciousness. He had accepted help from the hands that strangled Lorraine,
and felt contaminated as this room had been contaminated by Milne's use.

There was a photograph of Milne, very sleek and
athletic in a sport shirt, in a leather frame on the
dresser. He stared at the smiling face in cold anger
and confusion, unable to understand why Milne had
brought him home in the first place. Certainly humani-
tarianism wasn't the reason. It was possible, as anything now seemed possible, that Milne had intended to
kill him and had changed his mind. The intricacies of
the brain that hid behind that smooth face and vain
smile were completely mysterious to him.

Now was the time to call the police if he was ever
going to call them. A runaway man could disappear in
Los Angeles County for weeks or months, or forever.
No one man, searching alone, could begin to cover the
hotels and motels and apartments, the rooming houses, flophouses, call houses, where Milne might hole
up. A perversion of chance had led him to Milne
once, but he hadn't the slightest hope that it would
happen again. It was a job for the police, and even
they might fail at it.

He started for the telephone in the living-room,
wryly aware of the dramatic fitness of calling the police
from the fugitive's own apartment. Before he got to
the telephone he realized that, drama or no drama, he
couldn't go through with it. He didn't owe obedience
to Paula, but he owed her some kind of loyalty. Her
role in the case was too doubtful to permit him to
bring in the police.

His mind balked when he tried to define that role,
and understand her relation to the dead woman and to

Harry Milne. He had always thought she was honest,
almost more honest than it was natural for a woman to
be. Perhaps that was simply one of the illusions of
love. The pain and doubt of the past day had eaten
away some of his love for her, and he had come to feel
that he knew her less. He could no longer follow the
thoughts that moved behind her candid eyes. He knew
that she had been disingenuous, if not deceitful, in
urging him to think of the future, forget Lorraine, and
drop the case. But the Medusa fact that stood between
him and the telephone was worse than simple deceit.
She and Harry Milne had met before. Because Paula
had suppressed the truth, whatever it was, it followed
that she was obscurely leagued with the murderer. He
was afraid that if he looked further into that twisted
fact and saw all its implications, it would turn him to
stone.

He used the telephone to call a taxi, and went
downstairs to wait for it at the curb. When the taxi arrived he gave the driver Paula's address. As they
crossed to Wilshire in a rapid chaos of traffic his mind
went on working, half against his will. Paula was involved with Milne, perhaps in something connected
with the murder; by suppressing her connection with
Milne, she had been protecting him; in spite of her efforts Milne had been forced to run; there was a
chance that he'd run to Paula for further protection.

They turned into her street, a typical Hollywood
residential block of houses too elaborate and big for
their lots, sentried along each curb by rows of palms
like giant old men with ragged beards and their withered hair in their eyes. He saw Paula's car in her
driveway, and told the taxi driver to stop before they
reached her house.

"2245 is on up the street," the driver said.

"I know. Just stay here and I'll pay you for the
time."

They parked across the street and a hundred yards
short of Paula's house, and settled down to wait. The

driver stretched out diagonally in his seat with the exaggerated abandon of a man relaxing on the job. Bret leaned forward tensely with his elbows on his knees and watched the house.

After what seemed hours he looked at his watch. Ten minutes to six. No one had appeared on the glassed veranda or at any of the windows. No cars had come or gone. The declining sun made deep shadows between the houses, and the heat dropped out of the air as the shadows of the palm trees lengthened. The wide, low house where Paula lived seemed stable and peaceful in the amber light, washed clean and mellow by the gentle passage of time. A spray of water from the sprinkling system caught the horizontal rays and made a transient rainbow among the shrubbery on her lawn. Then the windows on the west side of the house burned ardently with borrowed light for the last few minutes before the sun went down. When the light withdrew, the windows were blank and dull like eyes that have lost their vision.

As the afternoon changed into evening Bret sank further into depression. It was a grim task he had set himself, spying on Paula's house like a detective or a jealous husband, waiting for the worst to happen. During the months he had been rebuilding his mind from its wreckage, it was Paula who had given him hope and energy to work against the inertia and boredom that oppressed him. She had provided the central meaning for the jerry-built thing he had made. His mind retreated in panic from the edge of the ruin he foresaw if Paula should be lost to him, the desert of dry ashes where he had lain once for an eternity bound hand and foot by paralysis of the will, in the undawning twilight of a mood too weak and cold to be called despair, prostrate in the chilly grip of self-disgust, obscurely plagued by little stillborn motivations, without reaction even to the memory of terror.

In those first months at the hospital, which telescoped in his mind into one gray undeviating day, he had been worse than dead, a useless shape of organic matter too feeble and sick to bear the psychic burden of humanity. From such unpromising material, time and the doctors and Paula's love had made him into a man again. Still he carried the memory of the ruin within him like the seed of a melancholy perennial. He had suffered enough to know his strength and weakness, and he knew that without Paula his world would turn gray again and bleed away to dust.

Yet he didn't see how he could help himself. He had to know the truth, and he had to see justice done. If he believed, as Paula said she did, that there was no justice anywhere, he wouldn't be able to go on. Without justice, human decency, human life itself, could not exist; and it seemed to him that his belief in justice depended on the outcome of this case. It was the one event in his life that presented the problem of justice in uncompromising terms, in spite of the fact that he himself wasn't entirely guiltless. If he had gone straight home and stayed there on that unremembered May night, still blank in his memory with the utter and tantalizing blankness of the empty frame that once enclosed the familiar portrait of a forgotten face, if he had stayed at home and waited for Lorraine, there would have been no murder, or he would have died preventing it. Failing that, he had to bring her murderer to justice, no matter what suffering ensued to Paula or to him. If Paula had conspired with Milne against his wife he had to know about it. He cursed his obsession and the ironic luck that had made him what he was and wedged him in this dilemma. But he stayed where he was, watching Paula's house.

The twilight was like a color blindness that leached off the colors of the roofs and windows and removed the third dimension that made the buildings real. The sky was still flamboyant in pink and yellow deepening into green, but night was lodging in the shrubbery and trees, in the corners of the houses, and under the eaves. A car appeared at the end of the block and came toward him, pausing twice before it stopped in front of Paula's house. It was an old, battered coupé, with a middle-aged woman at the wheel. When she left the car he could see that she was decently dressed but in some way dowdy looking, perhaps because the skirt of her dark suit was too long or her hat was too straight on her head.

Walking a little uncertainly on her thin legs, the woman crossed the sidewalk and approached the glassed porch. She glanced short-sightedly in the direction of the water spray and made an unnecessary and fussy detour. He was too far away to see her well, and the light was failing, but Bret felt sure he knew her. He knew in advance how she would climb the steps to the porch, her back straight and her head high, but with an awkwardness that came from fear of falling.

Paula came to the door before the woman reached it, and greeted her on the steps. They shook hands formally. The woman held herself a little shyly, as she always did. As always, Bret felt vaguely sorry for her. When the two women went into the house, it was not Paula but the other woman whom he followed with his eyes. Yet he had no idea who she could be.

In the back seat of the cab in the gathering darkness he wrestled with the dread that his memory was leaving him again. His head throbbed where the bottle had struck him. Perhaps his brain had been physically injured, his memory centers knocked out for good. The thought that had oppressed him throughout his convalescence came back and weighed on him heavily. The mind was tethered to the body like a sinful spirit cursed to spend a lifetime in a beast, absolutely dependent on such perishable stuff as human flesh.

CHAPTER EIGHTEEN

In spite of her rather unfortunate experiences with Professor Taylor, her first husband, and a bookish man if ever there was one, Mrs. Swanscutt had never ceased to be a lover of books. Anything between two covers, she freely admitted to her customers, was simply fascinating to her. It was this passion of hers for the printed word that had originally given her the idea of opening a lending library. It was a sort of literary thing to do, and it was a ladylike occupation. With her fine taste in books and her subtle tact in handling people, she hoped it would be profitable. God knew that after Frank was unjustly fired and they lost their house, they needed the money.

She didn't make a mint of money from the library, but to the secret surprise of a woman who had never before quite succeeded in anything, she made enough for the two of them to live on. When the war came, her business increased still further, and she became quite prosperous. Of course money wasn't worth as much as it used to be, but Frank had to admit that his scatterbrained little wife was making more money every week than he himself ever had. But he wasn't the sort of man to sit in his tent and sulk about it; he was

too much of a man for that. Since he couldn't very
well go out and take another regular job—his asthma
was still troubling him awfully, no matter what they
said about the California climate—he came into the
shop nearly every day to help her with her work. He
was especially good at keeping the books in strict al-
phabetical order according to authors' names, and at
counting the money.

In spite of all his illnesses and disappointments, the
poor dear always kept himself beautifully well
groomed too, and Mrs. Swanscutt was proud to have
him in the shop. She knew that many of her female
customers took real pleasure in being advised in their
choice of books by such a distinguished appearing
man. A lesser woman might have been jealous on occasion, but not she, not she. In every word Frank said
to her, in every look that passed between them, it was
so beautifully evident that he loved her as ardently
now as he had in the beginning. She still felt, after
twenty-five years, that her world had been well lost for
love. Good name, husband, and son—she had given
them all up for Frank Swanscutt, and he had not
failed her, he had not been unworthy of the sacrifice.

Still, she sometimes permitted herself to wish, in no
complaining spirit, that Frank could manage to come in
more regularly, and perhaps a little earlier in the afternoon. After the noontime flurry, business became very
quiet during the first half of the afternoon, and Mrs.
Swanscutt was suffering increasingly from boredom.
Six days a week for five years she had sat flanked by
books from nine in the morning till six in the evening.
Until recently she had tried to keep up with all the
best sellers in order to have an informed opinion, but
the last few months she had to admit that something
was happening to her feeling for books. Sometimes she
had to literally force herself to open up the front of a
new book and read the first sentence on the first page.
More and more she tended to rely on the publisher's
blurbs and the thumbnail reviews in the *Retail Book-
seller*. She was like a person with a sweet tooth who

has taken a position in a confectionery shop and ruined her stomach.

It was really funny the lengths she'd go to avoid reading a book. There were no clients in the shop, and there probably wouldn't be until later in the afternoon, so she could afford to admit it to herself for once. This particular Tuesday afternoon she had cleaned her drawer, counted her change, manicured her left hand (Frank would do her right one in the evening), cut several hundred bookmarks out of that pretty blue paper, made out filing cards for the six new books that had come in that morning, and phoned Mrs. Wionowski to tell her that *Forever Amber* was now to be had if Mrs. Wionowski happened to be coming by that day. Just when she had run out of things to do, and was beginning to be afraid that she might be forced by sheer boredom to take a look at one of the six new books, the afternoon paper came and saved her for another hour.

She went through the paper from front to back and read everything in it: the front-page stories, the murders on the third page, the movie advertisements, the sports page, the comics, the local news, the society pages, the editorial page, the woman's page, the deaths and divorces, and the business and finance section. Then she started in on the classified ads. This was really her favorite part of the paper, and she naturally saved it to the last.

There was real drama in the classified ads, so much more actual and satisfying than fiction, and such infinite variety. So many homeless people looking for a house. A young couple that simply had to have a refrigerator on account of the baby. Doctors that specialized in diseases of men or diseases of women. Private detectives who would go anywhere and find out anything for a moderate fee. Most interesting of all were the personals, those cryptic fragments of life that could lead you off into romantic daydreams for minutes at a time. "Edie come home, Mother gladly forgives you" (what had Edie done?). "Jack and Sim, the deal is still on if you contact me before Thursday. Charlie." (A bank robbery? the black market? who could tell?)

The last personal in the column rudely thrust Mrs. Swanscutt out of her daydream and set her heart beating madly. "Bret Taylor," it said, "call me at Gladstone 37416. P.W."

It's fate, that's what it is, Mrs. Swanscutt thought. Here I've been reading these things all these years, eavesdropping on other people's lives, and now fate has beckoned me into the inner circle.

Then the habitual dullness of her life reasserted itself and told her this couldn't be happening to her. It couldn't be her Bret; such things simply didn't happen. Not to her. Yet Bret Taylor wasn't a common name; she'd never have chosen it if it had been. Well, there was one way to find out. She could phone that number, if she dared.

After a period of nervous hesitation, she dialed Gladstone 37416 with an unsteady forefinger.

A woman answered: "This is Miss West's residence."

"Hello," Mrs. Swanscutt said excitedly. "Did you—are you the party who placed an advertisement in the personals column? I mean—"

"One moment, please," the woman said. "I'll call Miss West to the phone."

Servants, Mrs. Swanscutt noted. Bret must be on friendly terms with some very good people, if it *is* Bret. But of course it's quite impossible that it is—

"Yes?" said another woman, younger than the first. "This is Paula West."

Paula West, P.W. She was right so far. "Did you advertise in the personals for a Bret Taylor?"

"Who is speaking, please?" The voice was careful and brisk. Quite a good voice, she thought. A lady's voice.

"My name is Theodora Swanscutt." She laughed nervously. "It used to be Taylor. Bret Taylor is my son."

"You must be mistaken, Mrs. Swanscutt. Bret's mother died a long time ago. It must be another Bret Taylor. As a matter of fact, I've contacted him, so it's all right."

"I see," Mrs. Swanscutt said dully. "Well, I'm certainly glad you found him. I was naturally misled by the similarity in names. I'm sorry to have troubled you —"

"Just a minute," Paula said. "I'm afraid I'm being terribly abrupt. But would you mind telling me your husband's name?"

"Why, no. Franklin. Franklin L Swanscutt."

"No. I mean your first husband. Your son's father."

"George," said Mrs. Swanscutt. The young woman was being brusque to the point of rudeness, but after all she had asked for it and she'd go through with it. "George Watt Taylor. He was a philosophy professor," she added, not without pride.

"Then you're not mistaken. That was his father's name. But I can't understand it. Bret said his mother was dead."

"Dead? Of course I haven't seen him in twenty-five years. Tell me, is he there now? Could I speak to him?"

"No, I'm afraid he's not. But I'd love to have you come and see me. I'm his fiancée. Can you come for tea?"

Mrs. Swanscutt said she could, and Paula told her how to find the house. Then Mrs. Swanscutt threw caution to the winds and closed the shop for the rest of the afternoon. She didn't even call Frank to tell him she was leaving, and though she hardly admitted it to herself, there was a certain satisfaction in not telling him. Just let him come to the shop and find her gone, just let him wonder! She felt quite careless and gay in a way she hadn't felt for years.

Paula waited in a state of uncertainty and fear, as one might wait to keep an appointment with a ghost. The dead past was springing to life in unexpected forms. The banished years were coming home from exile to roost under her eaves like homing birds. Bewilderment and excitement turned her head, but a deeper emotion dragged at the bottom of her consciousness: terror. Bret had told her that his mother was dead, not only since his crack-up, but long before when they first met. Evidently he had been harboring a delusion for years. His insanity—for the first time she permitted herself to think of his illness as insanity —went far back, to their first weeks together. And how much further would it go? Ever since the night of Lorraine's death she had comforted herself with the belief that his mental condition was a temporary illness, an effect of shock that would wear off as its cause receded in time. But now she was uncertain.

Mrs. Swanscutt's telephone call had crystallized the fear that had been growing in her mind, that Bret was permanently insane, in spite of all her efforts lost beyond redemption. She was afraid, afraid for him and beginning to be afraid for herself. Two Daiquiris and six cigarettes did nothing to anaesthetize her fear. She had done all the wrong things, made all the wrong decisions, and that was the surest guarantee that she'd go on doing and making them right up to the final smash, whatever that would be. Her knowledge that she deserved whatever punishment she was going to get only deepened her fear. Every time she moved she made a misstep. Every time the telephone rang it suggested a new and dreadful possibility.

Her mind went round like a demented squirrel in a cage and gave her no peace. She went to the kitchen ostensibly to talk to Mrs. Roberts about dinner, actually to hear the sound of a human voice. Her housekeeper spoke calmly and cheerfully about the standing rib roast she had managed to get hold of, and whether she should go to the trouble of making Yorkshire pudding, but Paula could hardly listen to her.

"Do what you like. As a matter of fact, I'm not hungry. You might as well save the roast."

"But it's in the oven," Mrs. Roberts said firmly. "If I take it out now, it'll dry out."

"So what? Let it dry out!"

"You've got to get some food in your stomach, Miss West. I don't like the way you been eating lately. You may think you're feeling jittery, but going without your regular meals just makes you feel jitterier."

"Yes, I know. Go ahead and cook the roast. I've got a friend coming in for tea, by the way. I don't know just when, but she should be here soon. I'll let you know when to make it."

"It's a little late for tea, isn't it?"

"That doesn't matter." Afternoon tea was a habit she'd picked up from the English writers in the studio. It was a convenience rather than a ritual, something to do with the mouth and hands when cocktails were inappropriate or doubtful.

"Okay, Miss West."

Paula fled from under her friendly critical eyes, back to her living room. She tried to read a trade magazine, but that was a laugh. She couldn't bear to listen to a record. She couldn't even look at her Modigliani on the wall. Damn doll face! El Greco was more in her line at the moment, but she wasn't in the El Greco bracket yet, and probably never would be. If she got out of this with a whole skin and her nervous system all in one piece, she'd be having more luck than she deserved. "Funny," she thought, "a little while ago I was trying to talk Bret out of thinking about justice, and now I'm thinking that way myself." But the only alternative to justice was blind chance, something you couldn't face for long, not if you loved someone. So she was the girl who not so long ago had thought she could tear down the patterns of chance and rebuild them to suit her better. Now chance (or was it justice?) had taken the play away from her. If there was no Hays Office in the real world, there were no scenarists either—no human ones at least.

She heard the faltering engine as the car turned the corner and came down the street, and she was at the front door before the woman got out. A yellow taxi she had noticed when she glanced out of the window an hour or so earlier was still parked across the street near the corner. It occurred to her for a panicky moment that someone was watching her house, but she rejected the notion. She couldn't see anyone in the cab but the driver sleeping behind the wheel, and he was probably just snatching a couple of hours' rest after a hard day.

She stepped out onto the porch to meet Mrs. Swanscutt, who was climbing the steps a little uncertainly. There was something of the ghost about her, and something of the bird. Of ill omen? No, rather a timid bird listening for signs of danger; a hesitant, unwanted ghost looking for a house to haunt, with no assurance that she would ever find one. But that really wasn't fair. There was something appealing about her, in spite of her nervousness and thinness and the dating of her clothes. She must have been nearly fifty—she'd have to be, of course, if she was Bret's mother—but there was still a beauty of feature discernible in her sallow face. Paula looked into it for traces of Bret, and saw the same high-arched nose and blue eyes. There was none of his strength there, but there was a kind of vague charm hiding beneath the surface, almost as if it were afraid to show itself. There were lines around the mouth and eyes which showed that she had acquired the habit of suffering.

Paula liked her and felt sorry for her. She held out her hand and received the pressure of long thin fingers. "I'm very glad to see you, Mrs. Swanscutt."

"It was so nice of you to ask me over." She flung a bright birdlike glance upward at the house, as if to praise and glory in its size. "Coincidence certainly does have a long arm, doesn't it?"

She gave Paula a similar look of admiration, which was a little absurd but not unpleasant. One dressed for those looks from other women.

Mrs. Swanscutt herself was not well dressed, though the gray suit she was wearing had probably been smart enough when she bought it six or seven years ago, and she knew how to wear clothes. Time had flattened her chest and thinned her legs, but her bones were good, and she carried herself like a lady—a lady in adversity.

"Please come in." Paula led her into the living-room. "I'm sorry Bret isn't here. I know how eager you must be to see him."

"Oh, I am. Are you expecting him today? Where does he live?"

"No, I'm not expecting him. He's in the Navy, you see—stationed in San Diego."

"In the Navy?" Mrs. Swanscutt said brightly. "I'm so glad to hear that—he's doing his bit."

"He's had quite a distinguished career in the Navy," Paula couldn't refuse that to the woman, though a funny kind of grief was gathering in her own throat. "Wait a minute. I have his picture."

"I'd love to see it."

Paula ran upstairs for her framed photograph of Bret. He'd had it taken when he was first commissioned as an ensign, and he'd aged a lot since then, but it was the only one she had. Tears came to her eyes for some reason when she faced the young, smiling face on her dressing table. She wiped them away and went back downstairs to the living-room.

"That's my Bret," said Mrs. Swanscutt. "My, he's handsome, isn't he? You didn't tell me he was an officer."

"Yes, he was an ensign then. He's a full lieutenant now." In order not to postpone the inevitable she added: "He'd be in line for lieutenant commander if it weren't for his illness."

"His illness? Is he ill?"

"He's recovering, but he was seriously ill for a time. His ship was bombed last April, and he had an attack —" Her mind scrambled for the right word. All she could think of was "the screaming meemies," and that was what she had herself. She found it at last: "An attack of battle exhaustion."

"Why that's dreadful! The poor boy! But you say he's getting better?"

"Yes. Much better." I hope. I hope.

"Do you think he'll be glad to see me?" Mrs. Swanscutt said shyly. "Does he ever speak of me?"

"No, never." She was tired of handling people with kid gloves. Let them face the truth for a change, as she had had to face it. Irony and grief had already destroyed her sympathy with this woman, this sentimental mother who had forgotten her son for twenty-five years and now walked out of the past to claim her maternal rights. "Bret told me you were dead."

"That's strange. He couldn't have believed that. His father knew I was alive. He was a stern man, but surely he wouldn't tell his son that his mother was dead. It wouldn't be natural!"

It would be a relief to think it wasn't Bret's mind that was at fault, that he had been deceived by his father. But this idea, like a lamp turned on in the corner of a room, lit up one area while it cast the rest into deeper darkness. Dr. Klifter had told her over the phone that Bret had been deeply impressed by his mother's death. Yet his mother had not died. Could he have confused his mother with his wife? Stranger things had happened in case histories she had read.

"I may as well tell you, Mrs. Swanscutt, that Bret has had rather serious psychological difficulties. You couldn't have been in Los Angeles last May?"

"No. Why? We were visiting my sister in New Mexico. Do you mean that Bret had a nervous breakdown?"

"You might call it that—"

"His father had a nervous breakdown. That was before I met him, while he was still in the seminary. I don't think he ever recovered from it entirely. He was a very intelligent man, and highly cultivated, but he was always a little—unpredictable." She raised her voice slightly in sing-song defiance, like someone reciting a creed to a private god. "I've never regretted leaving him for an instant."

Paula took advantage of the opportunity. "Just what were the circumstances of your leaving him?"

Mrs. Swanscutt's blue eyes clouded and looked away. "It's rather a painful memory," she faltered. Then her voice regained its power and at the same time became a little phony. "Don't imagine that I consider that I did wrong. I followed the dictates of my heart, and I have never known a moment's remorse. I married Frank immediately after the divorce, and our marriage has been an ideally happy one. Our friends will tell you that. We put love ahead of reputation and convention, but a love like ours is more important than anything else, Miss West."

I know the feeling, Paula thought, even if your dialogue does need a little toning down (but then you learned to talk before Hemingway was here to teach you). "The last thing I want to seem is critical," she said carefully. "And I have no desire to cause you pain. It simply happens that Bret has been having trouble with his memory. He's confused about what happened to you, for one thing. It may be that if you tell me what actually happened it will help to clear up his trouble." She let out her breath slowly. Trying to get the truth out of an aging romantic was as ticklish as walking on eggs.

But the carefully chosen words had their effect. The woman looked both guilty and penitent, and she spoke in an honest, uninflated way. "I wouldn't have done anything to hurt Bret, not for the world. It was terrible for me to have it happen, and I hated to leave him. But he was so young I was convinced that he wouldn't remember."

"How old was he?"

"Four. He was only a baby. It couldn't have meant anything to him."

"Bret's doctor would probably disagree. I don't know whether you've read much about psychoanalysis—"

"Oh yes, I have. I do a great deal of reading."

"Then you know how important they think certain childhood events can be. Some of them say that the first year is the most important of all."

"I took very good care of him when he was a baby," Mrs. Swanscutt said irrelevantly.

"No doubt. But what happened when he was four? He told his doctor that he went into his room and found you dead."

"Is that what he said?" There was incredulous horror in the strained blue eyes. For a moment she might almost have believed that she had died then and had been deceiving herself for twenty-five years. Perhaps part of her died then, Paula thought, the part that belonged to her son.

"Yes, that's what he said. That delusion may be the origin of his mental troubles. That's why the truth is so important, do you see?"

"Is he in the asylum?" It was hard for her to say the word, but she got it out.

"Yes." After all, he had been in a mental ward until yesterday. She needed every available tool to pry the truth out of this misty-brained woman.

"My poor boy!" Mrs. Swanscutt said. "My poor boy!"

Mrs. Roberts came in with the tea cart, walking firmly as if she had waited long enough and was determined to get it over with.

"Oh, I'd forgotten about tea," Paula said, but she was furious. Damn Roberts for blundering in at the crisis of her third degree! And damn the Swanscutt woman for being a woman! She could guess well enough what Bret had found in his mother's room. But she had to know.

She said in a low hard voice over the teacups: "I believe you did Bret an injury, Mrs. Swanscutt. The least you can do is tell me what happened so that I can tell his doctor."

"I can't tell you. I can't."

Paula felt a cold fury gathering in her body. Once again she was fighting for Bret's sanity and her own chance of happiness. The woman could either tell her or get out of her house. "You had a lover," she stated.

"Yes." The admission was almost inaudible. "My

present husband. Frank was a graduate student in the college, and he did the heavy work around the house in return for a room. We saw a great deal of each other, and we fell in love. But you can't possibly understand the circumstances, Miss West."

"Why not? I'm in love—with Bret."

"After Bret was born my husband never came near me again. Do you understand me? He believed that intercourse was wrong except for the purpose of having children, and the doctor said I couldn't have any more children. George had his own room, and never once in four years did he come into mine."

I haven't bedded with a man for six years, Paula thought, but she didn't say it.

"Frank became my lover. I never thought of it as wicked. I simply didn't think of George as my husband any longer. He was more than ten years older than I, and he seemed more like a father to me after the first year. He was never ordained, but he was like a priest. Frank was my true husband."

"You needn't make apologies to me," Paula said. "Most of my friends have been married at least twice. I divorced my first husband in 1940."

"You did? For Bret?"

"No, I didn't know Bret then. For myself."

"I see."

The woman was stalling again. Perhaps she needed another jolt. Well, Paula thought, I'm the girl to give it to her. I take them, and I dish them out. "And when did Bret come into this? Or didn't he matter?"

"Of course he mattered." Mrs. Swanscutt said in her wispy, emotional voice. "I loved him too. I never dreamed it would turn out as it did."

"Yes?"

"He must have been frightened by a dream—he sometimes had nightmares, though he hadn't had one for a long time. Anyway, he woke up in the middle of the night and came to my room. Frank was with me. We were—in bed together. Bret came in very quietly and turned on the ceiling light—that was the first we knew of his being there. When he saw us he carried on something terrible. He set up a terrible howling and rushed at me with his fists. He bruised my breast quite badly."

I'm glad, said Paula to herself.

"George heard the disturbance and came running up the stairs. He caught Frank before he could get back to his room, and they fought in the hall. It was frightful. George knocked Frank down—he was quite a powerful man. I tried to take Bret in my arms and quiet him, but he hit and scratched at me like a wild animal. Then he ran back to the nursery, and that was the last I saw of him. George went downstairs and locked himself in his study. Frank and I left town that night and went to Cincinnati, where his people lived. Several years after that I received a legal notice that George had divorced me on grounds of desertion. Frank and I got married and came west, and I never heard from George again. Perhaps he *did* tell Bret that I was dead. I don't know."

Paula respected Mrs. Swanscutt's honesty, but it was not enough to keep her from hating the woman. She had harmed Bret, and that damned her forever in Paula's eyes. Still, she spoke as kindly as she could. "Thank you very much, Mrs. Swanscutt. Will you have some more tea?"

"No, thank you. But I do think I'll have one of these sandwiches. I'm quite famished." Her voice broke then, and she placed her hand lightly on Paula's arm. "I know you love Bret. You speak of him as if you loved him. Do you think I'm evil, an evil mother?"

"I think you were unlucky, I'm sorry for you. Bret was unlucky too—and George. He's dead, by the way."

The hall telephone rang, and Paula was there before Mrs. Roberts could come out of the kitchen. "Hello?"

"Is that you, Miss West?"

"Yes." She shut the door to the living-room with her foot.

"You know who's talking. I want to see you personally—now. Your boy friend has been sticking his nose in once too often, and I don't like it. Not a little bit."

"I warned you to leave town. You said you would."

"Maybe I did, but I'm not going, understand? I'm sticking around to see what gives. I think you've been giving me the cross, and I don't like it."

"Think what you like. I haven't."

"Maybe you haven't and maybe you have. Anyway, I want to see you. Do I get to?"

"Yes. Yes, I'll come. Are you at home?"

"Nix! Taylor drops in too much. I'm in the Mexicana Motel, room 106. Know where that is?"

"On Hollywood Boulevard?"

"Correct. I'll be waiting. And if you bring anybody with you you'll be making an ugly mistake—but ugly." He hung up.

Paula got rid of Mrs. Swanscutt as smoothly as she could, and backed her roadster down the driveway. At the last moment she ran back into the house to get the small .25 automatic she kept in the drawer beside her jewel case.

CHAPTER NINETEEN

It was dark when Paula's visitor came out of the house, but Bret was able to see in the light from the windows that Paula was not with her. The middle-aged woman got into her coupé and drove away alone. Bret had an impulse to follow her, if only to find out whether he should know her, but he decided not to. There was no reason to suppose that the woman had anything to do with the case or with him, and it was Paula he was following. He had a hunch that sooner or later Harry Milne would come to her or she would go to him.

The taxi driver woke up when the coupé went coughing by them. He stretched and rubbed his eyes. "Jeez! It's dark already. We going to be here all night?"

"Maybe. I don't know."

"I go off at eight, bud. It's past seven now."

"I want you to stay on if you can. Here's ten dollars on account."

"Well, I guess it'll be okay. But I got to call up the dispatcher."

"Not now. Wait."

A minute later, as if to verify his hunch, Paula's roadster backed down the driveway and stopped beside the front porch. She got out and ran into the house again.

"Drive down to the corner," he told the driver. "I want you to follow that roadster, but I don't know which way she'll turn."

"Right."

The taxi started up and rolled slowly past the house. Before they reached the corner the roadster backed out of the driveway and turned toward them. Bret took off his white hat and crouched down in the seat. The roadster, with Paula at the wheel, passed them at accelerating speed and turned at the corner toward the center of Hollywood.

"That's the one. Don't lose her."

"I'll do what I can," the driver yelled over his shoulder. "This jalopy is no speed wagon."

He kept the roadster in sight. It disappeared for a while in a traffic jam at Hollywood and Vine, but Bret caught a tail-end glimpse of it, and they gained on it again when it turned up the boulevard. After a mile or so it stopped at the curb, and Paula got out. They were in time to see her turn up the walk to the two-story stucco building with a red neon sign: "Mexicana Motel."

"Park up the street ahead of her," Bret said as he got out. "If she comes out before I do, watch which direction she goes."

"Okay," the driver said wearily.

Paula had avoided the door to the front office of the motel and had gone up a flight of open stairs on the left side of the building. As soon as she was out of sight Bret went after her. With his head on a level with the top step he saw her knocking at a door halfway down the balcony. The door opened, and for a moment he saw her profile clear in a shaft of yellow light. She went in, and the door closed.

Moving as silently as he could, Bret walked along the balcony, past a row of closed doors, to the one that had opened and closed. Enough light came into the courtyard to let him read the metal numbers on

the door, "106." There was a narrow window beside
the door, but the blind was tightly drawn. Not even a
human shadow appeared against the light, though he
could hear the murmur of voices. He stood against the
wall beside the window and strained his ears. There
was a man's voice yapping excitedly, and a woman's
softer tones. He knelt down and held his ear against
the window. Undoubtedly the woman's voice was Paula's, but he could not be sure of the man's.

The woman's voice rose suddenly, and he heard a
few words that made him sure.

"You'll keep your mouth shut or I'll kill you. . . ."
The man let out a mirthless hyena laugh.

Bret stood up and felt for the gun in his pocket.
Then someone spoke softly behind him.

"Hold it, friend. We don't want any trouble around
here now."

Bret whirled on a short egg-shaped man standing in
his shirt sleeves behind him with his hands in his pockets. "Who are you?"

"I run this place, is all. And what in hell do you
think you're doing?"

"Be quiet," Bret whispered tensely. Apart from the
danger in the situation he couldn't bear the idea of
having Paula come out and find him here. He moved
toward the man in shirt sleeves, who came with him in
the direction of the stairs.

"I saw you follow her up here. Your wife?"

"That's no concern of yours."

"Oh, yes, it's some concern of mine. You were all set
to make trouble, weren't you? Trouble is the one thing
my business can't stand."

They paused at the foot of the stairs, and the little
man's face shone ruddily under the neon. It was a
lined and drooping face, with thick black eyebrows
that pressed down on the squinting black eyes as if by
their own weight, a fleshy nose, heavy lips that
stretched insensitively around a dead cigar. The total
effect was ugliness and a kind of shrewd honesty.

"I can't stand here," Bret said. "She may come out any minute."

"So what! I thought you wanted to see her."

"Not her. The man."

"Come in here." He led Bret through a door marked "Office" and closed the Venetian blind over the front window. "What's the deal, Lieutenant? You trying to catch them *in flagrante delicto,* like they say?"

"No, nothing like that. Who's registered in 106?"

"That's the kind of information I only give to the cops—"

"Hell, I'll go and find out for myself!" He started for the door.

"Just a minute, just a minute. You want me to call the cops? I told you we can't stand trouble here."

Bret turned uncertainly at the door. "Who's in 106?"

"A guy called Miles. Checked in this afternoon. You know him?"

"I know him. Sorry, but I'm going up there."

The little man had been standing at the window peering out through the blind. "What's the use?" he said now. "She just came down a minute ago and drove away."

"God damn you!" Bret flung open the door to the street. Paula's roadster was gone.

"You said you didn't want to see her," the little man said behind him. "I didn't want you to, either. When you get a threesome with two sexes in it, it spells trouble. Trouble spells cops. Cops spell bad business."

"Keep out of this. I'm going up to see Miles."

"Maybe it'd be better if you didn't. You're feeling kind of overheated, aren't you, Lieutenant? I told you we don't want any trouble."

"Give it a rest. You've got to expect trouble when you rent rooms to criminals."

"A criminal because he laid your wife on you? Come on now, Lieutenant."

"This isn't a divorce case, you fool! This is murder!"

"What's that!"

Bret slammed the door in his face. The little man sat down at his desk and pulled his cradle phone toward him. He relit his cigar stub and blew several smoke rings. After a brief period of contemplation he crushed out his cigar and, without having used it, pushed the telephone to the back of the desk.

He then took a key case out of his trousers pocket, selected a small steel key, used it to unlock the upper right-hand drawer of the desk, and removed from the drawer a gray steel revolver with full chambers, which he shoved into his right trousers pocket. Then he went quietly upstairs.

CHAPTER TWENTY

When Paula came down the steps from the motel balcony she noticed the yellow cab at the curb. It seemed
to her that the driver's eyes were watching her covertly
from its shadowy interior. She kept it in her rear-view
mirror as she drove away. The cab stayed where it was
until she lost sight of it.

Evidently her nerves were playing her tricks again.
If they were, it was no wonder. The strain of facing
Miles and saying what she'd said had put her in a state
beyond fear. She felt hollow and light, like a blown
eggshell. She had poured out all her strength in sustaining that final stand, but it had worked.

Her only regret was that she hadn't stood up to him
months before. The money didn't matter to her, but
the last few months had eaten away her moral fiber,
and it was wearing awfully thin. She moved her hands
and feet and drove by the little sparks of life that hung
on flickering in her nerve ends. She felt too weak to
face the rest of the night alone, and she turned down
Wilshire in the direction of Dr. Klifter's hotel.

She phoned him from the desk, and he came to the
gate of the pueblo to meet her, a quiet-walking little
man in bright, informal clothes, with the air of a wiz-
ard in disguise.

186

"It is a pleasure to see you again, Miss West."

"I have to talk to you."

"Then walk into my parlor. Come." His English was remarkably pure, she thought absently, but his attempts to make gay little remarks gave him away.

When they were in his living-room he offered her a chair and a drink.

"I'm afraid a drink would make me drunk. Can you possibly give me coffee?"

"I make rather good Turkish coffee."

"Just some plain American coffee. Please."

"Certainly." He disappeared into the kitchen, and she heard the sounds he made filling the coffee maker. "Shall I expect Lieutenant Taylor tomorrow?" he called.

"I don't know." When she raised her voice it sounded dry and harsh. "He's walked out on me."

"Walked out on you?" The bearded face appeared in the doorway, complete in itself, like John the Baptist's head. She felt no certainty that it was attached to any body.

"He's trying to hunt down the murderer," she said unreally to the disembodied head.

"Yes?" The little trotting body followed the head into the room.

"He left me yesterday as soon as we got here. I saw him this afternoon. He'd been wandering around the city looking for the man. I tried to talk him out of it, but he was obsessed with the idea of finding the murderer. He said justice is more important than anything else." The room itself seemed disembodied now, a cube of soft light adrift in space, menaced by the jagged clamor of the stars.

"Perhaps justice is as important as that to him," said the other inmate of the wondering room. "His superego is remarkably strong, I think, even for an American."

"Superego!" she cried in the midst of bubbling laughter. "Can't you forget your jargon for five minutes? We're talking about a man. What right had you to tell him about his wife? It's had a terrible effect on him. He thinks he's found the murderer, and I don't know what he'll do."

Her uncontrollable laughter was suddenly displaced by tears. She covered her face and cried like a child. Klifter sat down and waited.

After a while she raised her eyes and looked at him. He was sprawled carelessly in a corner of the chesterfield, one arm over the end, his right ankle resting on his left knee. His trouser leg had crept up above his garterless sock, showing a pale and spindly segment of his right leg.

"I hear it boiling." He jumped up and went into the kitchen. "You wish it black?"

"Black, please."

He sat and watched her silently while she gulped the scalding coffee. It helped her to get rid of the end-of-the-world feeling she had had, the terrible immediate sense that the earth was whirling and plunging in open space. Wild dreams always had a whisky taste, but reality was bitter and hot and smelt of breakfast in her mother's kitchen in Highland Park, Detroit.

"Thank you," she said when he poured her a second cup. "If you'll show me where your bathroom is, I'd better fix my face."

Her faith in herself came back with the removal of eroded powder and the application of fresh lipstick, and her faith in the doctor came back along with it. When she returned to the living-room she told him about her visit from Bret's mother.

For the first time in their acquaintance she saw Klifter look surprised. "You are absolutely certain that this woman—what is her name?"

"Mrs. Swanscutt."

"You are certain that this Mrs. Swanscutt is really his mother?"

"No woman could act that part. No woman would want to. Anyway, what reason could she have for deceiving me?"

"I do not know. There are many things about this

case I do not know. There was no apparent reason for deception, yet your Bret has been a victim of deception for many years."

"His father must have told him his mother was dead. I can understand a man doing that under the circumstances."

"Yes, but he had a memory image, a pseudo memory, of his mother's death. He described the occasion to me in some detail. He said he went into her room and found her cold body, the hands folded on the breast, the head on a white satin pillow."

"I don't know what that false memory proves about his mind. If there's something irreparably wrong with his mind there's good reason for it. The thing he found that night must have been as shocking to him as death could be."

"Perhaps."

"I'm afraid I hate that woman," Paula said. "It isn't adultery I object to so much. It's the sloppy kind of adultery that couldn't be bothered to protect a child from its consequences."

"After twenty-five years the consequences have not yet ceased. I should have guessed the truth. I noticed those unreal elements in his story: the crossed hands, the satin pillow. Women do not normally sleep on white satin pillows, even in America. They do not arrange their hands in a funeral attitude when they die in their sleep. No doubt he saw the body of someone in a coffin when he was young—perhaps his aunt—and invented his mother's death scene from the material to satisfy his mind."

"But why should his mind seek that kind of satisfaction?"

"Evasion is a less clumsy word, and it may be closer to the truth. I cannot tell until I have talked with him at greater length and learned to know him better. He and I together must learn to know him. Still, let us suppose. Let us suppose that his father told him that his mother was dead. What might a small boy think? What might he not? He had blundered into her room in the middle of the night and found her doing something which he did not understand. It is very likely that he felt that in admitting this man to her bed his mother was cheating him of his filial rights. He ran at her in a childish fury and stuck her. Then the lover and the cuckold fought in the hall, and the little boy ran back to his own room. In the morning his mother was gone.

"Perhaps it was then, so soon, that his father told him she was dead. Death is a mystery to a child's mind, an awesome mystery. To us, too, it is a mystery, an inexplicable accident, but to a child! May he not have imagined deep in his heart that he had killed his mother with his feeble fists? Such a secret, too dreadful to be spoken of to his stern father, may explain the genesis of his guilt. All of us are guilty, plagued by anxiety and self-loathing, but there are some who are more susceptible to this than others. Your Bret has always been oppressed by guilt, and I think we may have found its source. If we can re-establish in his memory that strange night, that queer morning, we should free his mind of its burden."

"You can't," Paula said. She sat upright in her chair with her cup held steadily on her knee.

He stared myopically at her uncovered face. His white hands fluttered limply and returned to their perch on his knee. "You seem very certain," he said mildly.

"It seems to me that you're the one who's overcertain. You're explaining a man's life on the basis of very few facts, and even those facts are doubtful."

"All facts are doubtful. But consider my advantage. I have an actual witness, other than the patient, of the traumatic event, and that is rare in my work. I admit that my conclusions are hypothetical, subject to verification. But the immediate test of a hypothetical explanation is its power to explain, its impact on the imagination. I will state my hypothesis in more detail. The violence in the house, followed by his mother's disappearance and his father's silence, would be enough to convince the little boy that a great wrong had been done. It is easy for a child to suppose that he has committed a wrong. The line between wish and responsibility, between intention and guilt, is very thinly drawn in a child's mind. I do not insist that he believed he killed his mother. The possibility would be enough.

"No child could face such a horrible imagining for long. The mind protects itself in any way it can. A memory, or an imagined memory, which is too terrible to face must be pressed back into forgetfulness, covered up, and smoothed over. The boy's mind took refuge in the illusion that his mother had been dead when he entered her room. The violence was denied and forgotten. It was a harmless illusion, harmless except to him. While it enabled him to live and grow, free of conscience guilt, it planted the seed of guilt deep in his unconscious. It set the pattern also for his adult reaction to shock. Evasion at any price, at the price of memory itself. Does such an explanation explain nothing? Has it no impact of reality?"

"Yes, it does. It's dreadfully convincing. But does it mean, this pattern of evasion, that there is no hope for his memory?"

"On the contrary. It means that he must be told the truth. A man's life cannot be sustained on illusion doubly compounded."

"He must be told the truth?" she echoed. The question went on echoing in her mind until it embraced her whole life and threatened its foundations.

"I have thought so from the beginning. Now I am certain of it."

The lines of the conversation, spoken and unspoken, converged in a bright point of fear before her eyes. The point expanded into a vision of Bret, senseless and lost forever, slain by an arrow of truth. And where was he now? Wandering somewhere in the city, utterly vulnerable to evil. Entering a dark alley where a gunman was waiting?

She rose so quickly and awkwardly that her cup and saucer fell to the floor and shattered.

"It doesn't matter in the least," the doctor said before she could apologize. But he didn't rise to take the hand she extended. "Do not go just yet. Sit down again, please."

"I don't know where he is. I have to find him."

"Don't be afraid. There is no reason to be afraid. Circumstances struck at his Achilles heel, but he will recover."

"You don't understand. I'm afraid something may happen tonight. I'm afraid he'll get into trouble."

"I doubt it. I doubt that he will do anything wrong." His eyes seemed to have become brighter and smaller behind his spectacles. "It is true that the guilt-ridden are often predisposed to violence. Guilt is normally thought of as the result of sin, but it may also be its cause. A man who feels guilty may with unconscious deliberation commit an act which is sinful in his own eyes. Such an act may serve to rationalize his guilt, to justify it, one might say. Many criminals have performed senseless crimes, which could not fail to be discovered, in order to receive punishment for their guilt."

"It's ridiculous to talk about him as if he were a criminal." She was still standing in the middle of the floor. Tension and indecision had drawn her body off center and made her seem ungainly.

"Do please sit down, Miss West. Conversation is a sedentary art."

"I haven't time for conversation."

"But you must listen to what I have to say. And you must listen more carefully. I was speaking analogically and made no moral judgment on your Bret. I do not approach a case with moral preconceptions. I have argued with Stekel on occasions that an analyst should enter the patient's mind with no preconceptions at all. This case of Taylor tends to prove my point."

"How?" She sat on the edge of the chair, her feet among the shards of broken china.

"My preconceptions led me into error. I supposed almost from the beginning that Taylor was a clear case of infantile regression to the OEdipus pattern fixated by the mother's death. Now you tell me that the mother's death never occurred. That does not mean, of course, that the OEdipus element is not present. Taylor's relations with women will always be influenced, I had almost said determined, by his early relations with his mother. His sexual life will always be difficult because his mother betrayed him, so to speak."

"You don't have to tell me that."

"No. You are perceptive about these things. You must be aware also that in spite of his revolt against his father, he will always tend to see himself through his father's eyes. He cannot escape from the moral judgments which his father bequeathed to him. And with a part of his mind, the part which sits in judgment, he does not wish to escape."

"But wasn't his loss of memory an escape? You called it an evasion—"

"I know it. Perhaps there is a deeper explanation however. The loss of memory may have been a punishment inflicted on him by his own mind. A kind of death, a capital punishment."

"He said that," Paula whispered. "He said it was like death."

"Really?" He leaned toward her, his body a bundle of sharp angles loosely clothed in tweed. "Then the possibility is decidedly worth exploring. It raises a further question. What guilt, real or imagined, would require the self-infliction of such a punishment?"

Leaving the question hanging unanswered in the air, he leaned back against the arm of the chesterfield. Paula watched him intently, unable to relax. Without a cup to hold on to, her hands were playful in her lap.

He went on in his gentle, slightly thickened voice. "I have sometimes thought that we of the Viennese school have paid too little attention to problems of moral guilt. Freud himself was a child of his century. He never quite outgrew the physiological laboratory and its atmosphere of materialistic determinism. It is curious, is it not, that the subtlest introspectionist since Augustine should have under-valued the moral and religious life and seen the human mind in terms of blind forces working in Newtonian space?"

"You're talking like a Jungian," she said. "I can't listen to a lecture now."

He ignored her protest. "I am far from being a Jungian. I am an analyst first and always. Jung has reverted to type and abandoned analysis for theology. I think that explains his popularity in the United States, which has its own Calvinistic tradition. Nevertheless I must admit that the products of this moralistic tradition, men like your Bret, cannot be studied in a moral vacuum. They must be interpreted, partly at least, in their own moralistic terms. The guilt of such men cannot be taken for granted or explained away on general grounds. It must be traced to its source."

"But you explained Bret's guilt. You said that childhood experience was the crucial one." She rummaged in her bag for a cigarette, which broke in her fingers when she tried to light it.

He brought her an ash tray and remained standing over her. "The strains and shocks of the adult life are equally crucial in a case like this. You questioned my wisdom in telling him of the murder, but I maintain I was right. He must be told everything. To a mind which has been starved of truth, you cannot dole out truth in fragments. I do not know what you know. I do not need to. But he does. He is groping in the darkness of the external world for a truth his own mind has refused him. You tell me that he thinks he has found the murderer of his wife. Do you believe that he has?"

Two deep lines formed on either side of her scarlet mouth and twisted it like a pair of pincers. "I don't know. I—"

"Are you sure that you don't know? If you are suppressing the truth you are perpetuating the darkness of his mind."

"No!" she cried. "I've been protecting him."

"From reality? From justice? In ignorance he will find no justice. There is justice in the truth because they are the same thing. Would you deny him justice?"

"I have no faith in justice."

"But he has. Perhaps you do not need the faith. He does. When a mind has broken through the surface of appearances, a strong rope is needed to pull it out."

"I don't trust any rope." She felt the symbolic horror of the word and suppressed a shiver. "Do you, Dr. Klifter?"

"Have I faith in universal justice, do you mean? No. But I trust the faith of men who have it."

She sensed his weakness and thrust her wedge further into the opening. "Is that scientific? I came to you as a doctor, but you're talking like a priest—a priest who has lost his own faith."

"Very well, I accept the role."

"Though you yourself believe in nothing?"

"I believe in one thing: the individual man. I am not so mad as to try to remake men in my image. I remake them in their own."

"Even then you assume a great responsibility."

"No greater than the one you have assumed. I believe your responsibility is too heavy for you."

After a while she said: "I know it is."

"Then give him back to himself. Tell him the truth. I think he knows it already but will not recognize it. Eventually he will recover all his memories. When he does he will cease to trust you."

"I don't care about myself. I've lost him no matter what I do." She rose with a movement of disconsolate finality, gathering herself to face the outer loneliness and darkness.

He followed her to the door and gave her his hand. "Perhaps you have lost him. If that is so, his loss is the greater one. But I wish you both good fortune. You need not be afraid that I will tell anyone what I have guessed—not even him, if you do not wish it."

"Thank you." Her face was troubled but bold.

She went out, and he heard her heels click rapidly across the paved terrace into silence.

CHAPTER TWENTY-ONE

Bret knocked on the door of 106. After a heavy pause Miles called out: "Who's that?"

Bret knocked again.

"Who's there?"

Bedsprings creaked, and quiet footsteps crossed the floor of the room. The blind on the window beside the door twitched slightly. Bret flattened himself against the door. He couldn't see the window from there, but he could see the pencil of light that was thrown across the balcony when the edge of the blind was lifted. After a moment the light was erased.

The footsteps came to the door. They were hardly footsteps at all, but the muffled whisper of stockinged feet. Miles spoke softly through the door. "Is there anybody there?" A slight nasal wheeze added an overtone of uneasiness to the question.

Bret stayed where he was and said nothing. The door between them was so thin that he believed he could hear the other man's breathing. Very softly a hand touched the door and moved against it. A bolt screeched faintly as it was withdrawn from its socket. The knob on which Bret's hand was lightly resting turned against his palm. It was like a movement of repellent life in an unexpected place, a worm in the apple, a snake under the pillow. He removed his hand and stood back a few inches from the door.

Quarter inch by quarter inch it opened. A single eye blinked through the crack, unfocused. Bret forced his shoulder through the opening.

"You!" Miles said, straining against the door.

With his back against the jamb Bret forced the door inward with his hands. Miles stepped back suddenly, and Bret, unbalanced, came headlong into the room. When he looked up, Miles was facing him with his right hand in front of him on a level with his navel, his thumb pressed down on the base of a four-inch knife blade that projected horizontally.

The shining blade in its center brought the room into focus: the unrelieved ugliness of the stucco walls and the cracked ceiling; the uncarpeted floor worn through to the bare wood by endless traffic between the bathroom and the bed; the chipped metal bed with its frayed cotton bedspread crumpled in the central depression of the mattress; the single lamp on the bedside table wearing its scorched brown paper shade askew. No one came to such a room to live. You came to sleep for a night when nothing better was available; to escape from marriage or convention or police; or to wait. A pair of shoes on the floor and a coat draped over the only chair were the sole signs of occupancy. Miles had come here to wait, and the knife provided the meaning for which he and the room had been waiting.

Bret put his hand in his pocket and found the butt of the gun. "Drop it!" he said.

"You got no gun." His tone was half questioning.

With his forefinger curled snugly between the trigger and the guard, Bret withdrew his hand from his pocket and answered the question. Mile's eyes, the balance of power, the focus of the room, shifted to the more potent weapon.

"That I should get the cross from her!" Miles said. "A dirty double-crossing bitch like that!" His face contorted monkeylike in a strange combination of senility and childishness. "Sure, sure. Now tell me I'm talking about the woman you love."

His body was crouched and tense, but the knife, deprived of potency by the gun, hung down in his hand.

"Drop the knife and close the door."

Miles looked down at the knife as if he had forgotten it. He compressed the spring, shut the blade into the handle, and tossed it onto the bed. He went to the door, circling Bret with Bret turning at the center of his circle, and took hold of the knob with his left hand. For an instant his body was quite still.

"You wouldn't make it," Bret said. "Shut the door and come here."

When Miles turned from the closed door he was greatly altered by fear. His face was pale and seemed to have lost flesh. His carefully brushed blond hair was growing limp and dark, falling down over his temples like an adolescent's. His mouth had lost its shape and was feeling for another shape. Bret hadn't noticed before how wide and dark his nostrils were. A little thing like that could spoil his boyish good looks and give a corny touch even to his terror. A little thing like that was crucial when you were deciding to kill a man.

"What do you want?" Miles said. His voice was unsteady and high.

"Come here."

Miles moved toward him slowly, as if the gun projected a tangible force against his body.

"Stand still." Bret raised the hand that was holding the gun, so that Miles was looking directly into its muzzle. His eyes strained and crossed but could not look away. Suddenly his face was shining, streaming with sweat. Dark patches of wetness appeared on the breast of his shirt and under his arms. His whole body was realizing the fear of death. "No," he whispered. "Jesus!"

"How long did you know my wife?"

"Me?" he babbled. "I didn't know your wife. What makes you think I knew your wife?"

"Answer me quickly."

"We were friends, that's all. Just friends. She was a sweet kid. I never did anything to her." His roving eyes were drawn back to the steady gun. "Oh, no," he said. "Don't shoot." Two deep-curved wrinkles formed at the base of his nose. His teeth chattered between them. "You're crazy," he stammered.

There was a souring smell in the air. There was a sour taste in Bret's mouth, a sour sickness in his stomach. In the moment of triumph everything had turned sour. He was ashamed of his triumph, ashamed of the quality of his opponent. This chattering, sweating boy had violated his bed and killed his wife, but now he offered no resistance, no challenge. That wet shuddering softness was a sick anticlimax to the danger he had expected.

But the man had killed and the man had to die. He sighted along the gun. Miles saw the movement of his eyes.

He went down heavily on his knees. "Oh, God, Mr. Taylor, don't shoot! I told her I wouldn't bother her any more. It's all off, finished. You'll never see me again."

Bret stepped back a pace. "You told who you wouldn't bother her? Miss West?"

"Yeah, sure. I *promised* her."

"Were you and she in this together?"

"Yeah, but I told you it was all off. You don't have to worry about me any more, Mr. Taylor. I'll give her back the money, all of it I got left. I'll do anything you say."

For a sick and ugly moment Bret's hand had squeezed on the trigger, trying to fire the gun. It was what he had come here to do. It was what Miles deserved. But he could not do it. He had never shot an animal in the field, and a man was harder to shoot, if only because he had a greater capacity for fear than any animal. His years in the Pacific had given him an insurmountable backlog of sympathy, of fellowship with fear. As the fever went out of him he realized that he had no right to impose the fear of death on anyone.

"Get up," Bret said.

Miles watched the lowering arm, the gun declining from the level of his head toward the empty floor. He was still on his knees, but his posture seemed less abject.

"Get up. I'm taking you to the police."

"You can't do that!" Miles yelped. "They got my handprint. It'll put me in the gas chamber."

"You'll get what you deserve. I told you to get up."

"You take me to the cops, and I'll spill everything. Everything, you understand? You may be crazy, but you're not that crazy."

This is the end of Paula, he thought, of everything we planned for the future—the end of Paula and the end of me. But he could not kill Miles, and he could not let him go free. "Get up," he said.

Miles sprang toward him instead, his two hands at Bret's ankles and his shoulder crashing against Bret's knees. Bret went down on his back with a thud that knocked out his wind. His hand squeezed the gun in reflex. It fired once, then clattered on the floor somewhere behind his head.

Miles's hands were working up his body, pounding his stomach, tearing savagely at his face, closing on his throat. Bret jerked his hips, upward, unseating the man astride him and twisting onto his stomach. The hands returned to his throat from behind. Lowering his head, he brought his knees under him, straightarmed the floor, and rose to his feet. Miles was still behind him with his left arm hooked around his neck, his right fist pounding his kidneys.

He dropped to his knees again, jerking Miles forward and down with him, and reached up for Miles's head. He found it and took hold. Miles came over his shoulder, somersaulting in the air, and struck the floor with the full length of his body. But he was quick. Before Bret could pin him he was away and turning at the wall.

Bret looked for the gun and couldn't see it. A blow on the side of his face turned him around and sent him staggering to the other side of the room. Miles was after him before he recovered his balance. A heel in the small of his back slammed him against the wall and brought him to his knees with the feeling that his body had been broken in two. The second kick caught him a glancing blow on the nape of the neck. His head crackled and went numb, though he could still feel the raw half of his face that the rough wall had abraded. He twisted on his knees in time to receive the third kick in the stomach.

Miles closed in on him then, striking rapidly at his face with both fists. They hurt, but they didn't rock him hard. That was wonderful. Miles was fast and tricky, but he couldn't hit. All he had to do was take the punishment and concentrate on getting to his feet. The trouble was that his legs were hard to handle. And he couldn't concentrate on them properly with those fists in his face.

He flung himself up and out, trying to butt with his head. Miles stepped back just far enough and cuffed him to the floor with a rabbit punch. He rolled sideways and felt the iron leg of the bed against his head. Then Miles was behind him again, and the hands were at his throat. Bret caught hold of an individual finger and bent it backward. Miles sighed, and the hands went away.

Bret rolled onto his face, got his knees under him again, and raised the weight of his body with his legs. Miles caught him on the point of the chin with a long uppercut, almost before his hands had left the floor. He staggered backward, but his legs held him up. The man could not hit. That was wonderful.

"You can't punch," Bret tried to say. He discovered that his mouth was too numb to be used for speaking. He put his left fist in front of it, cocked his right, and moved in on Miles on his badly disciplined legs.

Miles waited for him, watching his feet. Bret feinted
with his left awkwardly. Miles countered and came off
balance. Bret's right struck him heavily in the neck
just below the ear. Miles backed away, stubbed his
heel on the wall, moved sideways along it. Bret followed him.

"You're finished," Bret said. "I'm going to spoil
your face for good." He had to speak elaborately, like
an elocutionist, in order to form the words.

Miles was no longer watching Bret's feet. He had
noticed his own left hand. Its second finger projected
rigidly, bent back at a right angle with the back of his
hand. He whimpered.

Bret hit him between the eyes with all his force. He
felt the bones move in his right hand, grinding against
each other like stones in a bag. Miles was sliding down
the wall inch by inch, his face turned sideways and his
eyes fixed.

Bret walked to the bed and lay across it. The cold
metal of the knife handle came in contact with his face.
He pushed it onto the floor with a weary gesture. All
his remaining energy was going into an effort not to
be sick. The sickness was pressing upward from his
stomach into his throat.

There was a slight movement on the floor behind
him the rustle of cloth against wood. Slowly he
raised himself and turned. Miles was squatting in the
corner with the gun. The flow of time stopped suddenly, like a river frozen in an instant by incredible cold.
For the duration of the endless moment Bret looked
into the muzzle, the dark, round mouth from which,
like a roaring word of command imposing silence,
death would come. All the traffic of his mind passed
through that narrow hole, the rat hole through which
his life, like a rodent fleeing from a collapsing building, was going to leave his body. Yet he was too tired
to be afraid, and too certain that the end had come, to
try to change it. He had found what he was looking
for, and he had hoped for nothing more than this.

Then the moment ended. Another moment began, and he was still alive.

Someone knocked on the door with an object heavier than a fist.

Bret said: "Come in," without turning his head. He was dizzy with the effort of continuing to live, but all his muscles had tensed for action.

"Stay out of here," Miles yelled. "I'll shoot."

"Stand back from the door," a man's voice bellowed. "We got a Tommy gun."

"So you brought the law, you bastard!" Miles was snarling. "I warned you." He fired at Bret.

A fraction of a second ahead of the bullet, Bret rolled off the bed onto the floor.

A loud stuttering sounded from the balcony, and a series of irregularly spaced holes made an inverted V in the middle of the door. Miles fired at the door. Bret rolled to the wall and lay still.

"Drop your gun and come out with your hands on your head," the voice commanded. "This is your last chance."

Miles fired again from the corner and started for the door of the bathroom. The rapid fire of the submachine gun began again, and a row of holes marched across the door and the opposite wall. Miles fell to his knees in a little cloud of plaster dust and crawled the rest of the way to the bathroom door. At the threshold he fell on his face and stopped moving. Bright arterial blood spouted from his mouth.

"You got him," Bret called. "You can come in."

The door was flung open. For a moment it was quite empty, framing the quiet night. Then a uniformed policeman stepped in, carrying his Tommy gun in the crook of his arm. Behind him came the little man who ran the motel, and another armed policeman.

Bret sat up with his back against the wall.

"What's your name?" the first policeman said.

"Taylor."

"And him?"

"His name is Miles."

"You mean it was."

Bret got to his feet and looked across the room. He had enough strength left to feel sorry for the dead man, enough strength to regret the loss of all the human blood that had run out on the floor. The rising sickness took him unawares. It doubled him over the bed, flooding his throat and mouth and nasal passages with bitterness.

His enemy was dead. He had accomplished what he set out to do, but the only taste it left in his mouth was bitterness. His mind was as sick and turbulent as his body. His closed eyes looked down into a seething darkness that extended to the bottom of the night. Even there he found unreality, a shifting unreality that tugged at the foundations of his mind, and the reflection of a face he was afraid to recognize because it was so much like his own.

"What a mess!" the first policeman said.

"I was afraid they were going to make a mess," said the little man.

CHAPTER TWENTY-TWO

The house was locked and dark when Paula reached home, but she felt no fear of going in alone. Having conquered the terrors of her mind and made her decision, she was immune to fear. Still, there were little things that continued to bother her. She was ashamed of having left the house without telling Mrs. Roberts that she wouldn't be back for dinner. In fact she was even hungry. She turned on the lights in the front hallway and went through to the kitchen. Mrs. Roberts had written her a note in bold black capitals and left it on a chair in the center of the kitchen floor:

> *Regret you did not see fit to eat dinner.*
> *Roast is in refrig. wrapped in wax paper.*
> *S. Roberts.*

She found the roast and made herself a sandwich. She wasn't jittery any more. She felt quite mistress of herself in a spinsterly way; a little cold and dead, but that was to be expected. She had elected a permanent spinsterhood, and it was no laughing matter. The thing she had chosen tasted very much like despair. It was as tasteless as unbuttered bread. Still, there was a certain satisfaction in getting your teeth into a solid chunk of despair.

She might have known from the beginning that it wouldn't be a laughing matter. He hadn't been merry in La Jolla; probably he had never been merry. His first kiss had been fierce and blocked, no gaiety in it. Even in love he was a man who moved with a weighty fatality, as if he meant everything he did and meant it forever. It was hard to believe that such a man could be so mixed up inside, still nursing a wound he had received when he was a baby. It was harder still to believe that mere words, even truthful words, could straighten him out and heal his wound.

Watch it, West, she said to herself as she munched her grief-stricken sandwich. You've made up your mind to go through with it and you're going to go through with it. No rationalizing, please. No more thinking at all. You haven't the brains for it, girl. And on the other hand you mustn't let your feelings be your guide. They made you what you are today. Just do what the doctor said.

She turned off the kitchen lights and went to her sitting-room in the front part of the house. There she settled down to wait for Bret. She had no reason to feel sure that he would come, but she had that feeling. She had only to put in so much time, and then he'd have to come. While the hands of her watch crept round past ten thirty and then eleven, she put in time.

Waiting was the one thing above all others that she couldn't stand, and she'd had so much of it lately. There were the months of waiting for him to come back after his ship went out from San Diego. More months of hopeless waiting after he married Lorraine. The worst months of all, suspended between mortal terror and boundless hope, while he was in the hospital in San Diego. She was still waiting, though the thing she had waited for had shriveled up and blown away. There was no more suspense, no more heights or depths. Her mind swung only in a little arc between the hope that he would come soon and the wish that he would not come for a long time. Even waiting was less painful than the end of the waiting was going to be.

She tried some music on the record player, but it stirred up her emotions, and she didn't want that. Emotion made the whole thing so real. She switched it off and listened to the silence in the house: the ringing deafness, the sound of time moving slowly through silence. You could hear it advancing step by step with your heartbeats, drumming you through the virgin country of despair.

One thing about despair: it didn't make you cry. You cried at its first onset, when you didn't really believe it. You cried afterwards perhaps, when you felt like starting to live again and found out that you couldn't. In the dead center of despair you couldn't cry if you had to. And that was a good thing, for crying puffed up the eyes.

The hands of her watch crept round to eleven thirty while she listened to the silence. She turned out the lamp beside her chair and watched the darkness too. Darkness and silence suited her quite well, but she'd trade them in for oblivion any day. You couldn't work, love, and suffer for years without feeling a letdown when it was all off at the last minute. Without, in fact, wishing you were dead. There was some slight consolation in knowing that time was grinding away, and you were on the assembly line, and the finished product was oblivion.

When she heard the car come into the street she knew that it was Bret. She'd have been quite as certain if it hadn't been. She ran to the front door and flung it open. When she turned on the porch light her heart jumped. It was a police car at the curb. Bret climbed out slowly and stiffly, as if his body had aged years in a few hours.

"You all right now, Lieutenant?" a man's voice called from the car.

"Yes. Thanks." The police car drove away.

She ran down the steps to meet him. When he came

into the shaft of light from the porch, she saw the gauze bandage on his face and forgot everything else.

"Darling, what's happened? Where have you been?"

"At police headquarters."

"But you're hurt."

"A little. Miles is dead."

"You—?" She felt her lips go cold.

"I didn't kill him," he said quietly. "I tried to, but I didn't. He was shot resisting arrest."

She put her hand on his arm to help him up the steps, but he moved slightly so that her hand dropped away. They went into the house in single file like strangers, with her following behind. She saw the torn seams at the shoulders of his blouse, the dirt on his back, the great blue swelling at the base of his skull. She almost sank to the floor before she reached a chair.

He turned on a floor lamp and sat down opposite her. She was keenly aware of the space between them, and of the alienation it symbolized.

"Miles's fingerprints checked with the prints on Lorraine's table," he said. "He was the man that was with her."

She tried to speak, but all she could hear was the voice babbling in her head: it's over then, it's over, I needn't ever tell him, and Klifter said he wouldn't if I forbade him. She had permitted indecision to enter her mind again, and it tied her tongue.

"You were paying money to Miles," he said then. "What were you paying him for?"

So it wasn't over after all. Well, it was what she deserved for going back on herself. In the end you got what you deserved.

"Do the police know?"

"I'm the only one that knows."

She gathered all her courage together in her throat and said: "I have something to tell you, Bret."

"I know you have."

He sat motionless, watching her. She looked directly into his eyes and was unable to assess their meaning. They were bright and steady and hard, unsoftened by love or any kind of hope.

"Miles was blackmailing me," she said with difficulty. "At first he threatened to go to the police. When I realized that he wouldn't dare, and told him so, he said he would go to you, and I couldn't let him do that. I've been paying him regularly for months. Tonight I saw it was no use. It had to stop. I went to him and told him I was finished. He tried to bluff me, and I did some threatening myself. I frightened him. It was easier than I expected it to be."

"He must have been frightened to do what he did. He tried to shoot it out with the police. But they had a machine gun."

"Were you with them?"

"I was with him in the motel. He tried to shoot me before they killed him. In spite of that I felt sorry for him when he died."

"You needn't have. He wasn't worth it."

"You did your best to protect him from me."

"I was afraid that you would kill him."

"Are you sorry he's dead?"

"I'm glad he's dead. But I'm gladder still that you didn't kill him."

"I tried to. I aimed the gun at his head and couldn't pull the trigger. I didn't know why I couldn't. Perhaps I felt I didn't have the right. I didn't have the right, did I, Paula?"

She started visibly at the challenge in his question. She looked into his face again and understood the meaning of his eyes.

"You remember?" she whispered faintly.

"I think I have a pretty clear idea."

The scene that flickered at the back of his mind was dimmer and more confused than his firm voice admitted. It was shadowy dark like an underexposed film, and all but erased by other pictures superimposed upon it. He saw himself in the scene, small and foreshortened and faceless like an unknown actor whose movements have been recorded by an overhead cam-

era. The faceless man in blues, dwarfed by the high
May night, went up the walk and into the white bungalow. Another man, half out of his clothes, ran across
the unlighted living-room, through the kitchen, and
out of the house. Lorraine was in the bedroom trying
to cover her body. Darkness covered her body.

He knew what he had done, but he had no memory
of the act. He drew his knowledge of it from the emotions that still poured along his nerves and stained his
blood with their acid juices. Outraged self-righteousness and its hot and dangerous anger, the savage wish
to inflict pain on the source of pain, the hopeless desire, which lay like an eyeless worm at the core of
murder, to end an impossible situation by violence.
The very violence that stretched it out forever.

Paula watched his eyes turn inward and lose their
sight, fogged once more by the obscurity at the center
of his life. He looked as if he had forgotten her completely, and it frightened her. Complete indifference,
nothingness, was the one enemy she had no idea how
to fight. Any kind of talking was better than this long
blind silence, even the kind of talking she had to do.
She invented the desperate hope that if she could join
him there, link hands with him in his darkness, they
might emerge together on the other side.

"You asked me to tell you," she said.

"Yes?" He spoke almost absently, like a man just
coming awake.

"I wasn't with you when you found Lorraine."

"I know. I remember."

"Lorraine wasn't dead when you found her."

It was terribly hard to say. She could feel the sweat
gathering in drops between her breasts and trickling
down to her waist, leaving a cold trail. It was terribly
hard, and why was it up to her? How did she come to
inherit a job like this? But that was too easy to answer.
She'd asked for it. Everything she'd done, she'd done
because she wanted to. It was her baby, and she knew
it.

She felt giddy and light when he took it away from her.

"I know I killed her. You needn't temper the wind to me. But I don't understand what happened. You must have known I killed her."

"Yes," she heard her voice replying from some corner of the room.

"And that was what Milne knew, that was why you were paying him?"

"Yes."

"You shouldn't have put yourself in his hands."

Her sense of herself came back from a great distance, and her voice came with it. "I did what I thought I had to do. After that it was too late to change anything. I had to go through with it."

"I don't understand why. Tell me what happened." The part of his face she could see was rigidly controlled, and his firmness gave her courage to go on.

"I wasn't there. I came when you telephoned. I only know what you told me over the phone and what Miles said afterwards. You told me that you were in dreadful trouble, that you'd found Lorraine with a man, and killed her. When I got to your house you were unconscious in the bedroom. Lorraine's body was on the bed."

"But you said you spoke to Miles. I thought he ran away."

"He did. They saw you coming up the walk, and Lorraine knew you. Miles came to see me the next day. He'd read about me in the papers, and realized that I had some money and that I'd lied to the police. I've been paying him ever since."

"I had to drag you into it, didn't I?" His voice cracked and became raw with emotion. "I wasn't content to make a filthy mess of my own life. I had to drag you into it."

"You made me glad," she said. "You called on me to help you when you were at the end of the rope, and it made me glad."

Before the love and courage that shone from her tired face, he felt a terrible humility. Not the false and transient humility of wounded pride, but the humility a man who has lost and regretted his virtue feels in the presence of virtue.

"I'm not fit to live in the same world with you, Paula. This afternoon I even suspected that you and Miles were partners in some way."

"I know you did. It's no wonder you were suspicious of me. I lied to you, I lied to everyone. When the police came I told them the story that you and I had been for a drive, and that we were together when you found Lorraine's body. Once I'd told that lie I couldn't change my story or they'd have thought we conspired to murder. It's strange, isn't it? They never doubted my word."

"No one should ever doubt your word."

"That's the hell of having an honest face," she said. "If I'd been challenged I'd have had to tell the truth. Nobody challenged me. I know now I should have told them the truth anyway. Considering the circumstances, you might have been acquitted or given a short manslaughter sentence. But I waited until it was too late. Then I found out that you didn't know yourself what you had done. I was afraid of what the truth might do to you. But I was wrong about that too. I did the wrong thing from start to finish."

"No."

He was so deeply moved that he couldn't say anything more. Shame washed over him like waves of dirty water that left him foul and breathless. He was sick to death of himself, the self-deluded fool, proud and intolerant and hard of heart, who had projected his own guilt outward like a shadow that darkened everything it touched. Phrases from his childhood came back to him like fragments of a language he had almost forgotten, or was just beginning to learn. The mote that is in your brother's eye . . . the beam that is in your own. Judge not lest ye be judged.

He was no more than a tiny mote of darkness in

the sun, a little seed of flesh thrown down between th earth and sky, blown here and there by the wind of time that swept away the insect generations of men. He had betrayed his own side in the unequal war against death, and deserved nothing of anyone. Yet he drew a bitter strength from his humility. He could say the word "murderer" to himself and answer to the name. He could see it was not justice but mercy that he needed.

He leaned forward and covered his shamed face with his hands, so that his words were muffled. "You took such a risk for me. You must have been crazy to think I was worth it."

" 'Crazy' is a word we don't use in our family." She tried to smile, but her mouth was forced into a grimace of pity instead.

She couldn't bear to sit here and see him bowed. She crossed the space between them and went down on her knees, holding his head to her breast. She felt his body shaking and held him tighter. She would have liked to be able to divide her own flesh, to take him inside of her and shield and comfort him.

"What am I going to do?" he said against her breast. He had taken a life and could no more evade his guilt than a hunchback could unstrap his hump. Whatever he said for the rest of his life would be censored by the knowledge that certain things could not be spoken. His perceptions would be darkened forever by the black memory that stood between him and the sun. Yet there was no way out. He couldn't tell the police, for if he did, Paula, who was innocent, would suffer for his guilt. He had to go on living with the knowledge of what he had done, not just tonight, but every night, and in the daylight. "What can I do?" he said.

"Come to bed. You're tired, and it's past midnight. There's nothing for you to do but come to bed."

"Can you possibly still love me?"

"Tonight before you came I thought I'd lost you. I wanted to die."

"But aren't you—?" His voice broke.

She held him tighter still, as if her arms could smother the remorse inside his head. "Aren't I what?"

"Afraid of me?"

For a second she felt quite panicky, she didn't know exactly why. She wasn't afraid of him, but she was afraid. Life was so very complicated and unpredictable, and the energy she needed to cope with it had all drained out of her tonight. She'd been living on her nerve for months, buying vitality on margin, and all the bills had come due at once. She knew that she had won, but she was too tired to realize her victory, too tired to think of the future without fear.

No doubt she'd feel different in the morning. Life would begin again, and the unsettling future would become the routine present. There'd be people to see and dialogue to write, appointments with Klifter, meals to plan, a place for Bret to start to work again, an excuse to put off Mrs. Swanscutt for a while. She didn't want that bird of ill omen at her wedding; it was already equipped with ill omen enough. Still, she was sure that things would get better. The worst of the danger was over, and the worst of the pain. Things would never be as good as they might once have been, but they would be good enough. She had learned not to make too great demands on life. It was enough for her at the moment that she and Bret were very close to each other. She told him without faltering that she could never be afraid of him—she loved him too much.

"You're very good," he said. The warmth of her body had penetrated to his marrow, and he wasn't shaking any more.

"Come to bed," she said again.

They went up the stairs arm in arm. It's past midnight, she was thinking, but it's still a long time till morning. To him she said more cheerful things.

ABOUT THE AUTHOR

Ross MACDONALD was born near San Francisco in 1915.
He was educated in Canadian schools, traveled widely in
Europe, and acquired advanced degrees and a Phi Beta
Kappa key at the University of Michigan. In 1938 he
married a Canadian who is now well known as the novel-
ist Margaret Millar. Mr. Macdonald (Kenneth Millar in
private life) taught school and later college, and served
as communications officer aboard an escort carrier in the
Pacific. For over twenty years he has lived in Santa Bar-
bara and written mystery novels about the fascinating
and changing society of his native state. Among his leading interests are conservation and politics. He is a past
president of the Mystery Writers of America. In 1964 his
novel *The Chill* was given a Silver Dagger award by the
Crime Writers' Association of Great Britain. Mr. Macdonald's *The Far Side of the Dollar* was named the best
crime novel of 1965 by the same organization. Recently,
he was presented with the Mystery Writers of America's
Grand Master Award. *The Moving Target* was made into
the highly successful movie *Harper* (1966). and *The
Goodbye Look* (1969), *The Underground Man* (1971)
and *Sleeping Beauty* (1973) were all national bestsellers.

THE THRILLING AND MASTERFUL NOVELS OF ROSS MACDONALD

Winner of the Mystery Writers of America Grand Master Award, Ross Macdonald is acknowledged around the world as one of the greatest mystery writers of our time. *The New York Times* has called his books featuring private investigator Lew Archer "the finest series of detective novels ever written by an American."

Now, Bantam Books is reissuing Macdonald's finest work in handsome new paperback editions. Look for these books (a new title will be published every month) wherever paperbacks are sold or use the handy coupon below for ordering:

WHODUNIT?

Bantam did! By bringing you these masterful tales of murder, suspense and mystery!

☐ 23282	**A RATTLING OF OLD BONES** by Johnathan Ross	$2.75
☐ 23498	**BLACK MONEY** by Ross MacDonald	$2.95
☐ 22618	**THE THREE ROADS** by Ross MacDonald	$2.50
☐ 23514	**THE DARK TUNNEL** by Ross MacDonald	$2.75
☐ 13449	**THE FEGUSON AFFAIR** by Ross MacDonald	$2.75
☐ 23140	**GUNS** by Ed McBain	$2.50
☐ 23130	**LONG TIME NO SEE** by Ed McBain	$2.50
☐ 20104	**MURDERS ANONYMOUS** by E. X. Ferrars	$1.95
☐ 20666	**MIND OVER MURDER** by William Kienzle	$2.95
☐ 20572	**THE WHITE PRIORY MURDERS** by Carter Dickson	$2.50
☐ 20375	**DEATH IN FIVE BOXES** by Carter Dickson	$2.25
☐ 20155	**THE SECRET ADVERSARY** by Agatha Christie	$2.50
☐ 23273	**ROSARY MURDERS** by William Kienzle	$2.95

Prices and availability subject to change without notice.

Buy them at your local bookstore or use this handy coupon for ordering:

Congratulations— But...

What about all those questions and problems that arrive with a new addition to the family? Here are several invaluable books for any new or expectant mother. They are filled with helpful hints for raising healthy children in a happy home. Best of luck and may all your problems be little ones!